HOOD FAIRYTALE

By Dashay Denise

Published by Cadmus Publishing LLC. P. O. Box 8664. Haledon, NJ 07538.

Web: Cadmuspublishing.com, BooksByPrisoners.com

Business email: admin@cadmuspublishing.com

Author email: info@cadmuspublishing.com

Phone: 360.565.6459
ISBN#978-1-63751-444-3

Book catalog info. Urban Life

CadmusPublishing.com

Prologue

We move towards the door and push it open without a sound. Still stepping lightly, we creep down the stairs and notice that Rah Rah and BJ are sitting around a table laughing and talking shit while they count up stacks of money. We hit the bottom of the stairs, guns ready, and they both jump up at the same time.

BJ attempts to go for his gun. "Don't try it, nigga," Shine's voice freezes him. "Get the fuck on the ground!" she demands.

Rah Rah laughs arrogantly. "Bitch, you better believe if you don't kill me I'm takin' out your whole muthafuckin' bloodline," he taunts.

Shine laughs in response. "I know how you move, nigga. You a dead man talkin' right now, and I don't fuck wit' the dead so-" She doesn't even finish her sentence before she lights his ass up and his body drops to the ground. Blood pours from his bullet wounds, creating a puddle underneath his body.

"FUCK! Y'all really killed my fuckin' brother, mane. Fuck!" BJ is crying hysterically. His pussy ass ain't built for this shit. Hearing the noise, Keno makes his way down the stairs letting off a couple shots from his own gun. I turn quickly and lay his ass to rest before he makes it to the last step and his body rolls the rest of the way down. BJ is still in rare form, screaming and crying like a newborn baby.

"Bitch, you next," I tell BJ, irritated by his whining. "We just need the code to the safe. And we'll be takin' all this," I point my gun in the direction of the stacks of money sitting on the table. Shine starts packing the money in duffle bags as BJ moves obediently towards the safe and begins putting in the code.

I turn away for a second to make sure Mookie is helping Shine load the money up, and don't notice BJ pull a gun out of the safe.

Pow!

Chapter One

Shine

It's my night to close. The clock reads 11:58 PM. Our last client just left out, so I sweep up around the station he sat at and make sure everything else is in place before I grab my car keys to exit and head home. Right on cue, as if she can feel me, my cellphone screen lights up with a message and a smile spreads across my face.

My Queen: *U hungry?*

Me: *U know I am baby. I'll be home in 30. Just closin' up shop.*

My Queen: *OK, see you soon.*

We've been in a real good place lately. I feel grateful for that knowing how stressful life can be at times. I've had a lot going on in other areas, so it helps to have a woman at home who can hold it down for me. She doesn't know I've still been in the streets. I promised her that I'd keep my hands clean and just make my money at the barber shop, but I want her to have the best life. I want us to have a family soon. That can't happen if we're just getting by.

After the last run-in I had with the law, I told her I was putting the streets behind me. I did for a while. But a few weeks ago I fell back into it. Some old friends wanted to hit a lick and they knew I was the woman for the job. I blend in well enough - my 5'3" height, caramel skin-tone with freckles, and low hair cut - hanging with a bunch of men, you'd never notice I wasn't one of them. My looks tend to get us in the door, but they don't only need me for that. I'm usually the brains of the operation. I get us in and out in minutes with very few errors.

We came up pretty good over the last few weeks. All of the money is circulated through the barber shop and a couple other small business I own to clean it. Afterwards, I set it aside in a separate account to give my queen the life of her dreams, our dreams. And what she doesn't know won't hurt her, right?

I lock up the shop and walk briskly to my car - a white Dodge Charger with all white interior - ready to get to her. I get in, crank up, and turn on the stereo system. J. Cole's track "Love Yours" plays through the speakers:

Love yours

Love yours

No such thing, no such thing as a life that's better than yours

No such thing as a life that's better than yours

(Love yours)

No such thing as a life that's better than yours

No such thing, No such thing...

A twenty-minute drive gives me time to think about how we got where we're at now. I think back to when we first met: *It was a year ago. She was dropping a friend of hers off to the barber shop, because her ol' man was there. I happened to look up as she got out of her car - all thighs and hips, no waist, long, brown, wavy hair that stopped at her ass which was just enough to grab on, but not too much - and walked to the hood of her car to sit while she chopped it up with her friend. I damn near skinned the middle of my client's head before I dropped the clippers completely.* Lord, have mercy, *I thought to myself.*

"Aye, who is that?" I asked my homeboy, Zach, who was lining his client's neck. I pointed out the window at her.

"Oh, dat's Travis's girl, Mya," he answered, making Travis look up to see his woman walking towards the shop. "She's coming to pick her man up from daycare." The shop erupted in laughter.

"Stop playin', nigga," Travis threatened.

"Sorry, bruh. You know dis a woman-free zone. She always rollin' up on you," Zach shook his head.

"I wasn't talkin' 'bout her anyway," I interrupted them. "I was askin' 'bout the white girl drivin' that Mercedez-Benz. Wassup wit' her?"

"Oh, she ain't keepin' time wit' nobody, man. You can hang it up. She keeps her nose up like she better than e'erybody. Like ain't nobody worth her time. Boujee ass bitch," Zach said in a salty tone.

"She must've friend zoned your lame ass, huh?" Travis countered, laughing at him for his attitude. All the shit talking of the barber shop faded out in the background as I watched her get back in her car gracefully and pull off. I didn't know much about her. I didn't even know her name. But I did know that one day she would be mine.

A few days later, I saw her again. She was leaving out of the nail salon that was across the street from the barber shop. It was about 10:30 in the morning. I made it to the shop late that morning, but looking back on it, I think it was no coincidence - destiny maybe, or fate. She stood at her car door texting for the longest and I finally got up the nerve to go holla at her.

I crossed the street, hardly looking both ways first, because I was so focused on catching her before she took off on a nigga again. When I got close enough, I took a deep breath and said to myself, Here goes nothin'. Don't fuck this up.

"Aye, ma, you from around here?" She looked up at me with indifference then glanced back down at her phone. Now that I had a close-up view, I could tell she was a little shorter than me, maybe about 5'1", and her eyes were honey brown.

"Damn, tough crowd, huh? Wha'chu say we chop it up over lunch, my treat?" I propositioned her with charming eyes.

"I'm sorry, do I know you?" she asked, sounding a little annoyed, but also a little curious. "Well, my name is Shyanne, but most people just call me Shine. And no, you don't know me, but I'm tryna change that part." I looked at her to gauge her impression of me, she rolled her eyes subtly and leaned her head to the side as if she had heard that line a million times before. "I know what you're thinkin' - I've heard that line before - *but maybe I can show you better than I can tell you." I could see the shift in her eyes.* And they said she was hard up they must not know 'bout me. I still got it.

"I'm actually busy today, so I can't do lunch," she responded as she opened her driver-side door and propped her elbow on it while looking at me defiantly.

"Well, dinner then?" She didn't say anything for a long minute, but finally I broke through her exterior and she agreed.

"Dinner? Yeah... I can do dinner. Here's my number," she took my phone out my hand and input her number to my surprise, "send me the location and I'll meet you at 7 tonight." She handed the phone back to me and got in her car, cranking it up and revving her engine before she zoomed off. Show off, *I thought while smiling and making my way back to the barber shop. I looked down at my iPhone she had saved her number and name - "Nevaeh (; "- heaven spelled backwards. I had a feeling she was about to have my whole world backwards too.*

I'll never forget that night. I was a little early arriving to the restaurant. I was dressed down in my best Polo attire, all black top to bottom including my shoes which were the latest edition of all black Ones, diamond studded earrings, a Presidential Rolex on my wrist, and a 16" chain of crushed diamonds - a silver angel wing hanging from it. I had picked a bouquet of red roses, trying to hint that I wanted a little more than just friendship with her. I paid extra to give us a more private setting - window seat with low lighting and smooth background music. There was a candle as the centerpiece of our table.

I don't know why I was nervous. I had had plenty of women in the past, most of them didn't go anywhere past good conversation and chillin' on late nights, but I was never nervous like this before. I tried to get ahold of myself, but all my efforts were lost when she walked towards the table. A red, satin, turtleneck dress with no sleeves and a slit up the left side of her thigh traced her curves she had on black Red Bottom stiletto heels, her hair fell down her back loosely, and she didn't wear very much makeup. Natural beauty. I had a good feeling about this one.

The night was effortless. It came to an end a little too soon for me, so I took her for a walk along the levee. We talked all night about everything and nothing at all. From then on, I knew I'd do well to keep her in my life I could only pray that she would stay. I came with a lot of shit. I hoped that was something she could deal with. But who knew, maybe I'd be willing to make a few changes for the right one.

I snap out of my flashback with the ringing of my phone. It was my potna, Lo. This dude has been hitting my line all day, so I guess it has to do with another lick. It has been really weighing on my conscious, the promise I made to Nevaeh to end this lifestyle. But maybe it won't hurt to go all out one last time.

I hit the green button. "Shine, nigga, I been callin' you all day, what's good? Can you get wit' us tomorrow night? This is the big one. Can't miss it, we gon' retire on this one, man, I'm tellin' you." he sounds hyped up.

"Man, this is it, for real. Y'all know I'm tryna get out the streets," I tell him, a sternness in my voice.

"Yeah, you 'bout to put a ring on that shit, we fuckin' know. Damn, this is it, a'ight?" he confirms.

"All right. I'm pullin' up to the crib now. Get everything together and I'll meet you tomorrow evenin' to talk details. We'll get this money and be on our way," I say as I back into the apartment complex's garage and park.

"That's a bet."

I hang the phone up and shake my head. I walk around to the front door of our apartment, and as I open it I can smell the good food my baby has prepared for me. When we first moved in together she was burning water. She came a long way. All those YouTube videos and cookbooks must've paid off. I slide my shoes off at the door and walk into the living room, throwing my keys on the table. Then I make my way to our kitchen. *Ours,* I love the sound of that.

Chapter Two

Nevaeh

In five minutes the homemade, baked macaroni and cheese will be ready to take out of the oven. Thank God for those YouTube tutorials, because I would be a long way from getting a ring on my finger if I hadn't upped my skills from the first meal I cooked for Shine. *Terrible* would be an understatement. I remember it like it was yesterday.

It was our first night living together in our new apartment, and when Shine walked in the door the smoke detector was going off loudly. I was standing on a step-stool, fanning the detector with a white dish towel while smoke was billowing out of the oven. The burnt-to-a-crisp chicken that sat in the baking dish on the kitchen counter was still sizzling. And when I looked up and saw Shine standing in the doorway with weary, big eyes, I just burst into tears. What was left to do?

To make matters worse, Shine started laughing. I mean, not just a little chuckle, but the kind of laughter that comes from deep within the soul. She left the door wide open to let the smoke out and walked towards me. I was a mess. She picked me up, cradled me like a baby, and discreetly took her cellphone out of her back pocket to order pizza and hot wings from Dominoes. The fire department called to confirm that there was, indeed, no fire, and once I was settled down, we cleaned the kitchen up together. By this time we were both laughing.

With a big smile on my face from that little flashback, I start setting the table for us to have our dinner together. With her running the barber shop, she comes in after midnight five nights a week. But we've always been more of night owls anyway, so I don't mind. Things are pretty quiet when she's gone. I work from home as an insurance agent. Most of the time, my work is pretty thoughtless. I just have to be available within my working hours to answer the phone and assist people with their insurance needs. I make pretty good money doing that, but it does get a little redundant. I am two years away from a Bachelor's degree. Once I finish that, I will be able to put energy into opening my own business.

Lately though, most of my focus has been on keeping myself healthy and stable. Shine and I have begun our IVF journey and the doctor is very adamant about me having as little stress as possible to make sure my body takes well to the embryo transfer. Since Shine has been keeping herself out of the streets, I've had very little to worry about. As long as I know that she's safe and will come home to me every night, I'm happy.

No sooner than I pull the macaroni out of the oven and finish setting the table, do I hear the door open. A smile crosses my face and I feel my stomach fluttering. We've been together for almost two years and she still gives me butterflies. I hear her keys hit the coffee table and her footsteps draw nearer to me.

"You're just in time, my love. The food's hot 'n ready," I call to her before she makes it to the kitchen. She walks up behind me and wraps her arms around me placing both hands on my flat stomach.

"I know something else that's hot 'n ready," she says in my ear before kissing me on the cheek and turning me around to face her. I clasp my hands around her neck and give her a kiss. "Smells great, babe. I'm starving."

"You had a lot of clients today?"

"Yeah, you can say that. Brought a good bit of money in though, so I can't complain," she says to me as she sits in the seat across from me. We say grace and dig into the food without many words in between.

When our plates are empty, I clear the table and rinse all the dishes before placing them in the dish washer. Not long after, I make my way to our bedroom. Our apartment isn't huge, but it's perfect for us. The living room is comfortable and the kitchen is a bit small for my taste, but it will do until we save up the money to buy our first house together. It has two spacious bedrooms, one master bath, and one half bath for guests. Our apartment complex is in a low crime area, which says a lot for Baton Rouge lately, because the crime rate has been through the roof for years now. But it's home. It's likely we won't be leaving anytime soon, so we're making the best of it.

Shine is in the shower already, so I grab the remote and surf through the channels looking for a movie to watch. There isn't much on, so I end up choosing *Friday After Next*. That movie never gets old. I am laughing so hard my eyes are watering when Shine finally makes her way to the bedroom. She's wearing nothing but her gray Niké sports bra and gray Niké boxer briefs to match. I keep my eyes on the TV screen, because I know as soon as I give her my undivided attention I will forget the TV is even on, and that's exactly what her mission is.

She walks around the bed to plug her phone charger up and sit her phone on the nightstand to charge overnight. I take a deep breath and bite my lip to contain my smile. *Why does she have this power over me?* I think to myself.

"What did I tell you about biting that lip?" she pulls me away from my own thoughts with her demanding voice. I look up at her and shrug my shoulders, trying to play innocent. "Yeah, you know what I told you. You seen that movie enough times to be able to recite all the damn words, so quit playin'," she sounds a little jealous. Such a turn-on. Then again, everything she does tends to turn me on.

"Don't come in here tryna give me a hard time, bae," I poke my bottom lip out, pouting. "I made sure you had a clean house and a cooked meal to come home to, so don't start your shit." I try to hold in my smile.

"You know what I really want when I come home?" she asks while looking me up and down. I have nothing on but one of her black, v-neck Polo t-shirts and a lacy, black Victoria's Secret bra and panty set underneath. Before I can answer her, she grabs me by my ankles and pulls my ass to the edge of the bed. I burst into laughter again, but I know this is about to get serious.

She let's go of my ankles, only to pull me in closer to her and I wrap my legs around her waist. She kisses me softly on my lips, before moving to my ear, nibbling and sucking there while she reaches around me to grab the TV remote. She switches to the media player on the Smart TV and chooses the "Makin' Love" playlist we made together. Soon the song "Hands On" by Trey Songs fills the room:

There's places on your body

You ain't even know til now

If you let me explore I'll help you find

Your way around ('round)

She continues trailing kisses down to my neck, while pulling my panties down my legs and tossing them to the side carelessly. I close my eyes, letting myself get lost in the moment. I start pulling my shirt up, but she takes over, more in a rush now to get to it. She throws my shirt in the same direction as my panties and with expertise unhooks my bra, tossing it as well, while laying me back on to the bed.

"This is what I want," she says seductively, lowering herself down between my legs, trailing kisses down my left thigh until she is kissing my lips. She uses her tongue to separate my pussy lips, tongue kissing and sucking my clit in an unnerving rotation. The music can hardly drown out my moaning. "You like that, huh?" she asks, stopping just long enough to watch me squirm under her grip.

"Yes, baby, don't stop," I say breathlessly, completely weak under her control. My legs are resting on her shoulders, while her right hand has a tight grip on my waist. Still twirling her tongue around my clit and pulling it slightly between her teeth, she slides two fingers into my pussy - in and out, in and out, in and out. She quickens the pace, putting more pressure behind her fingers and moving her tongue so fast that my body starts jerking under her grasp.

"I'm 'bout to cum, baby," I holler at her, she pulls her fingers out and, with both hands, grips my ass and pulls me into her mouth while my pussy juices start to flow and my toes curl. "Mmm," is all I can get out before I cum hard onto her tongue, the juices flowing down the crack of my ass.

"I see you missed me," she says pridefully, standing up straight and pulling me back into her arms.

"Is it that obvious? It's really not fair what you do to me," I tell her, putting my forehead against her chest, catching my breath.

"I just wanna please you, ma, only you, forever." She wraps her arms around me tight and kisses the top of my head before walking towards the closet door. I am more than ready for what comes next.

Chapter 3

Shine

———∽०୧ஓ౦∾———

With the taste of Nevaeh's juices on my tongue, I know I want more of her tonight. Hell, I might even take the day off tomorrow just to lay up in it all day. It's been a week since we went to the fertility clinic, so I'm hoping we find out that she's pregnant soon. Until then, I'm planning to fuck her like I'm putting a baby in her for real. I pull my red and black Niké backpack out of the closet where I keep my strap-on. I can see Nevaeh out the corner of my eye biting that lip of hers.

I take the strap-on out of the backpack and quickly step into the harness, wasting no time. I adjust it to fit snug, feeling Nevaeh's eyes on me. I walk back to her, positioning myself between her legs as I kiss her again.

"Tell me you want it," I say in her ear while sliding the tip of the dick up and down her slit, teasing her. "I want it." That's all I need to hear before I push into her. I keep the rhythm slow, breaking her in and going deeper with each stroke. Her head falls back as she wraps her legs around me and presses her fingernails into my back.

"Deeper," she moans, and I push all 8 inches into her pussy. With both hands, I grab her by her ass cheeks, picking her up and pressing her against the wall. I'm pounding her harder, faster, and deeper until she's screaming my name and throwing her pussy on me, matching my rhythm. The strap is hitting against my clit just right and I feel myself building up pressure, not wanting to cum yet.

"Fuck, I'm so close," Nevaeh yells while I suck on her neck, still thrusting inside of her. "It's right there, baby."

"Cum for me, ma," I tell her and with the last stroke, her legs tighten around me and her juices start to flow for me. I walk her over to the bed, she climbs out of my arms, and I turn her around roughly.

"Bend over." She complies and I push back in her as she braces herself with both hands on the bed. I lose myself in her, stroking her deep, and watching her ass as she throws it back on me. She bends lower, gripping both ankles and I grip her hips and grind into her. Her legs are starting to shake and I reach my right hand around her to play with her clit, moving my fingers against it in a circular motion.

"Ooo, baby, that's it," is all I hear her say before I reach my climax.

"Shit, Vae, I'm cumming," I moan and her legs are shaking uncontrollably while she cums with me.

***

After we get cleaned up and settle into bed together, it's about 1:30 in the morning. I get a text from Lo saying to meet him at Mookie's spot at 6 PM. I look over at Nevaeh while she's asleep. She really believes in me, in us, and I really hate to upset her. There's something about her being upset with me that unsettles my soul, but I know I have to do this. Once it's all over and she sees things went smoothly, she'll understand - that's what I'm hoping for.

I run my fingers through her hair and she seems to smile a little. I wish I knew what she was dreaming of, in her little fairytale world she lives in. I often tell her things aren't always rainbows and butterflies, but I do my best to protect her from the bad shit. All I want is to keep that smile on her pretty face. I respond to Lo's text, letting him know I will be there and place my phone on the nightstand before wrapping my arms around my queen and falling asleep.

Chapter 4

Lo

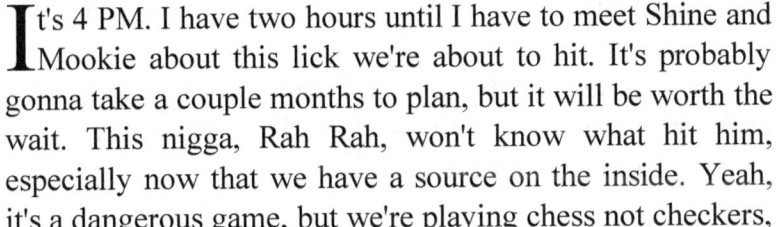

It's 4 PM. I have two hours until I have to meet Shine and Mookie about this lick we're about to hit. It's probably gonna take a couple months to plan, but it will be worth the wait. This nigga, Rah Rah, won't know what hit him, especially now that we have a source on the inside. Yeah, it's a dangerous game, but we're playing chess not checkers, and at the end of it all, we'll be saying *checkmate.*

I grab my truck keys off the hook by my front door and step outside, locking the door behind me. Gray clouds are rolling in to the left of me. I hope this storm coming in isn't a bad omen or some shit. I try to shake that thought while I walk to my truck - a black Ford F-150 with black rims - and open the driver's side door. Before I even have time to get myself situated, the sudden ringing of my phone startles me. I take it out the pocket of my joggers and answer the incoming call.

"Aye, Mookie. I was just 'bout to head your way in a few. What's good?"

"Not much, just wanted to let you know that Keno stopped by. I didn't let him get too comfortable though, he's gone now. We're a go on setting this plan in motion," she confirmed.

"Sounds good. See you soon, Mook," I said before ending the call and putting my truck in drive, slowly backing out of my driveway.

I have to make a quick detour before I head to this meeting. I know Keisha is missing a nigga and it's been too long since I seen her fine ass. I've been so busy grinding and getting to this bag, and I never want her to be involved in the streets if I can help it. She tries to be understanding, but I know she's getting tired of waiting for me to get my shit together. I just don't know if I can ever part with this lifestyle. I'm almost 30 years old and I know it's time, but I'm just not ready to settle down.

There's no need for me to call ahead to pop in on Keisha, because I know she wouldn't play with me with no other man in her crib. After about a 25 minute drive, I pull up to the apartment complex and park in an empty spot close to her apartment. I hop out my truck, making sure to hit the lock button on my key ring as I make my way up the stairs to her apartment door. I let myself in with the key she gave me and immediately the smell of fried chicken, fried okra, and collard greens fills my nose.

Just as I thought, I find Keisha in the kitchen standing over the stove, taste testing what I assume is the collard greens from a silver pot. I stand there quietly, admiring her physique. She's 5'6" tall, light-skinned, with enough ass to sit a wine glass on which is currently half exposed by her pink boy-shorts, and her perky 32B cup breasts are poking out of her black tank-top. Her body is perfection, plus she ghetto as hell - just my type - not to mention the bitch is bat shit crazy.

About a year ago, Keisha caught me with a chick from the block. Before I could even attempt to explain myself, she sliced my ass wide open with a switchblade. It left a nasty scar, but I guess you can call me crazy too, because I stayed with her. Love makes us do off-the-wall shit... and when you get caught with your dick in your hand, what else can you do but take your lick like a man.

She turns to grab a glass plate out of one of the kitchen cabinets, standing on her tip-toes to reach the highest shelf.

"Mmm-mmm," I clear my throat and she instantly shifts her body to face me as the plate falls from her hand and shatters on the floor.

"FUCK! Lo, you scared the shit outta me! What the hell is wrong wit' you, nigga?! How long you been standin' there?!" she goes off into a rant screaming at me. "You ain't been over here in God knows how long. Now you wanna come over here and let yourself in like you fuckin' live here. Gimme that key, 'cause you damn sure don't deserve it," she fusses, turning to grab a broom and dust pan to clean up the broken glass.

I watch her for a second before responding. "Look, I ain't tryna hear all that. I'm here now, Ke. Why you gotta be extra? You know what a nigga do to keep this money comin' in, so now it's a problem?" I shake my head and turn to walk out the kitchen, making my way to the black Lazy-Boy recliner in her living room. I slide my Retro 5's off my feet and prop my feet up, flipping the TV station to *NBC* to check the score of the New Orleans' Saints football game; the Saints are ahead, 14-7 at halftime. *At least somebody's winning right now,* I think.

"See! Look at you," Keisha says, standing in front of the TV so I can't see the screen. "This what you do, nigga? Giving me all these lame ass excuses... just get the fuck out!" She's pissed off, I get it though. It's kinda hard to listen to her complaining while I'm sitting eye level with her pussy print. *Damn, I miss that.*

"Are you fucking listening to me?! Get the fuck -"

I stand up and grab her by her throat, cutting her off mid-sentence. There's anger in her eyes, but at least she's no longer able to throw insults at me from that flip ass mouth of hers. I walk her to the wall and hold her in place with my grip tight on her neck. With my other hand, I pull her tank-top up over her breasts exposing them, and squeeze her left breast with my left hand, while sucking on her right nipple. She starts to whine and squirm a little under my grasp. I loosen my grip on her throat and she inhales deeply.

"You done wit' all that fussin'? 'Cause I'm tryna hear some different noises come outta you, baby," I say, pulling my shirt over my head and tossing it behind me on the recliner. In response, she slides her boy-shorts down her legs and steps out of them. I pull her into me and bend her over the arm of the recliner, licking my lips before kneeling down to eat her pussy from the back.

She's so wet already, tasting like water. I take her clit between my lips and suck on it before dipping my tongue in her hole.

"Lo," she moans, making my dick even harder. With one hand I pull my joggers and boxers down, using the other hand to finger her. Two of my fingers are sliding in and out of her pussy as she grinds against them. I don't hesitate to replace my fingers with my dick, pushing into her wet, tight pussy from the back and stroking her deep and hard, tryna reach her soul.

She screams my name again, throwing her ass back on my dick like she wasn't just cussing me out and telling me to leave. That's what I like. We've always had this love-hate relationship which makes the sex fire - rough and wild, just what I need right now. I'm digging deeper into her and her juices start running down my dick. I keep pumping, grabbing her long hair and wrapping it around my hand, pulling her head back while she moans so loud that I know the neighbors hear her.

"Fuck me harder, daddy," she says and I let the beast out, ramming into her like there's no end. "Harder," she cries. "Baby, I'm 'bout to cum." Her pussy tightens around my dick and she cums hard on my length letting out a heavenly sound of pleasure.

Seconds later, I pull my dick out and let out my seed all over her ass cheeks. No babies yet. We are not ready for that. Well, I'm definitely not ready. Keisha turns to face me and gets on her knees to lick the leftover cum from the tip of my dick, which only makes me rock up again. She takes me into her mouth, using her hand to cover the rest of my length and deep throats my dick like a pro.

"Fuck. That's it, Ke. Suck this dick like you own it," I say, eyes rolling back while I guide her with my hand on the back of her head. I push myself deeper in her throat and she doesn't gag at all. It doesn't take long and she's swallowing my seed as it's running down her throat.

"Oh, shit, bae." I moan as she sucks me dry and I pull her up from her knees to face me. "I love you, Ke. I know I been fuckin' up by not makin' way for you. I'ma do better," I tell her.

"I know," is all she says in response. She smiles at me, but her eyes show that she's still upset, even after that good dick I put on her. I don't have time to deal with that shit right now though, because I have to make it to this meet up.

"Baby, I gotta go." I grab my clothes, putting them back on while I look around for my shoes. I find them on the other side of the recliner and put them back on quickly.

"You *always* gotta go."

"Don't start. I'll be back in a few hours, OK?" She looks at me with uncertainty and pouts a little. "I'm coming back, don't trip. I gotta handle this business with my crew. I love you," I say, walking to the door to open it.

"Love you, too, Lo," she says as I close her door behind me, rushing down the steps and back to get in my truck. I pull out onto the road and head to Mookie's place. Five minutes later, I remember Keisha was just finishing up cooking when I pulled up on her. I pull my phone out and send her a quick text to make sure she puts me up a plate in the fridge. I know she's gon' make sure I'm good, always. I'm just tryna do the same for her.

It only takes about 15 minutes to get to Mookie's in Fairfield. When I turn onto Jackson Street, I shoot her a text to let her know I'm pulling up. She texts back to let me know that Shine is already there. Good. I put my truck in park and look up to see Mookie standing outside waiting to meet me. I meet her and follow her into the house so we can get straight to the business.

Chapter 5

Mookie

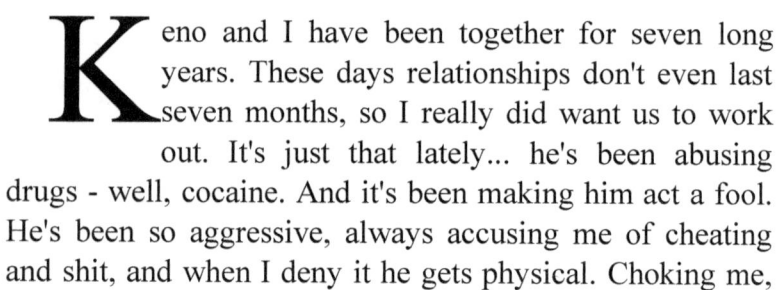

K eno and I have been together for seven long years. These days relationships don't even last seven months, so I really did want us to work out. It's just that lately... he's been abusing drugs - well, cocaine. And it's been making him act a fool. He's been so aggressive, always accusing me of cheating and shit, and when I deny it he gets physical. Choking me, slapping me, punching me... I really love him, but he's not himself anymore and I'm getting tired of his bullshit.

Which is why I was down with this plan. Keno is Rah Rah's younger cousin. Yes, the big-time drug dealer, Rah Rah. Keno was raised by his grandmother, but when she passed away, Rah Rah took him under his wing. He's been a corner-boy slinging coke for him ever since. And lately, that nigga can't go no more than an hour without snorting that shit up his damn nose.

After our last fight, I decided I was done with him. But I'm keeping him on a leash to make sure this plan gets executed on point. Rah Rah's trap house is on the dead end of 46th in Parktown. Ms. Kim, the lady living in the trap house to throw the feds off their trail, is a 57 year old black woman that drinks Vodka all day - straight out the bottle - and talks shit with the young boys who hang around over there. Since she's their cover up, nobody really suspects that the trap holds all Rah Rah's drugs and most of his cash. Who does know where it's all stashed is Keno, and that means: so do I. After all the shit he's put me through, you'd think his lame ass would be more careful about telling me all those secrets. *Right game, wrong bitch.*

"Let's get to it," Shine cuts no corners, getting straight to the point. "Wha'chu found out?"

"Keno been tellin' me all we need to know about the trap. We just gotta get in. So, this weekend he's bringing me to Rah Rah's and we gon' chill there for a few hours while they get all the inventory together," I explain to them.

"Security codes, entrance and exit points, we need all that," Lo says.

"Nigga, I know what we need. I got this," I tell him, rolling my eyes, because its typical of a man to underestimate a woman. "The main thing is knowing when his next delivery is coming in. We're gonna need to move in after that."

"We gon' get the drugs, the money, and off these bitches, right?" Lo asks, already knowing the answer.

"You know how we get down, no witnesses. No face, no case. I'll take care of the weapons and shit. Mook you gon' be in already, making sure the cameras are off and the doors are unlocked. In and out with no mess. Understood?"

Shine lifted her eyebrow, looking at Lo and I, authority in her voice.

"We good. I'm wit' it," Lo responded.

"You know I'm wit' the shits," I said, trying not to get too hype. I just want Keno out of my life so I can move on. *That muthafucka gon' wish he never fucked over me. Sorry ass nigga.*

"A'ight. I'm out. I gotta get back home," Shine pulled his phone out, checking the time. "Lo, get wit' me when Mookie has a date for the drop and we gon' meet to set it up."

"Bet. I'ma head out too, Mook. Hit me up when you know sum'," he nods his head to me before standing and heading for the door.

"I will.

"I see Lo and Shine out the door and head to the kitchen to pull a glass out the cabinet. I go to the alcohol cabinet and pull out a bottle of Hennessey - just one glass to take the edge off. My nerves have been so bad lately. I put my right hand on the back of my neck and rub the tension out. I'm sore from the last fight I had with Keno. I thought I needed to go to the hospital. I'm sure I have a fractured rib, but I'd rather bury him six feet under the ground, then put in a prison cell. Louisiana's prisons are overcrowded anyway, so what better way to rid the world of evil. Two wrongs don't make a right, but I don't give a fuck anymore.

I down the glass of Henney, feeling it burn a little as it goes down my throat. I walk down the dark hall of my house toward the bedroom. I start to strip out of my clothes and make my way to the bathroom to start running my bath water. Soaking in a hot bubble bath should soothe the pain of my body a little, just not the pain in my heart.

I walk up to the full body mirror in my bathroom. While I wait for the tub to fill up, I stare at my naked body in the mirror. I've always been a thick girl, but I've never really been self-conscious. My brown complexion is marked up with black and blue bruises all over. My eyes water a bit, but I refuse to let a tear fall. No more crying over this nigga, that's a done. He don't deserve my tears. I walk over to the tub and step into to the water. As my body lowers into the steamy, bubbly, lavender scented water, I close my eyes and picture bullets flying towards Keno's body - not one misses the target. *Rest in peace, bitch.*

Chapter 6

two weeks later...
Nevaeh

I t's been three weeks since the embryo transfer. I haven't heard from the doctor yet, but we should get a call any day now. My doctor's appointment is in eight days. I can't lie, I am extremely nervous, but I am trying to stay in a positive mental space. I have been taking all the precautionary measures the doctor suggested and Shine has been very supportive and present during this journey so far. I don't know where I'd be without her.

I was able to take the day off of work today. There haven't been many calls come in this weekend, so I gave myself a three day weeks and forwarded any calls to my assistant, Coryn. Coryn is new at the company, and though she is only 18 years old, fresh out of high school, she is learning quickly and turning out to be an asset here. She's been training to stand in for me when the time comes for me to take my maternity leave. I'm grateful to have her to count on with all that's going on in my life right now.

It's still early. The sun is just starting to rise, so it can't be any later than 6 AM. I don't hear any movement in the apartment, so I assume Shine is already gone. It's not unusual for her to leave early in the morning, but normally Friday is the day she leaves the house late. I wonder if something happened. The thought only dwells in my mind for a moment until I realize how badly I have to pee. I urge myself to get out of bed, because I know I won't be able to go back to sleep anyway.

After my normal morning routine is complete, I check my messages and remember that Ariana and I are supposed to be meeting at the nail salon at 9:30 this morning. I read her text reminding me of that and the thought of spending time with my best friend puts a smile on my face. I don't get to see her often. Between work, school, and putting so much focus on IVF and Shine, sadly I don't make time for my social life. I do miss the hell out of her though.

Me: *Thanks for the reminder, Ari - you know I wouldn't miss it.*

Ari: *Don't be late busy woman!*

Me: *I wouldn't dare, lol. See ya soon!*

Ariana has been my best friend since our first year of high school - *I was new in town and very weary of meeting new people. It didn't make sense to me to even attempt at making friends, because every year my mom met a new guy and we moved to a new city - which meant I enrolled at a different school. I was forever the 'new girl,' and it was tiresome. Fortunately, my mom got married my freshman year which I prayed meant that we were settling in one place for a while.*

It was seventh period, music class, and Ari was sitting off to the side away from the rest of the students. She was tall for a girl our age, thin, with shoulder length dirty-blonde hair. She was looking like she didn't exactly want to be in class that day, or in school period, but there was something about her that made me like her instantly. I sat in the empty seat next to her that day and every day afterwards. We were inseparable. Two years into high school, Ari dropped out of school to get her GED. She had found out she was pregnant and wanted to be able to support her child. She promised that her leaving school wouldn't change our friendship, but this was something she had to do.

Snapping out of my flashback, I start cleaning up around the apartment a little, putting things back where they go. I clean the coffee pot out and wipe the black marble countertops down with Lysol disinfectant wipe. I put a new cartridge of Ocean Breeze scented Febreeze spray in the motion censored dispenser on the counter near the garbage can. Before I head towards the bedroom to get dressed to meet Ari, my phone dings on the table alerting me that I have a text message.

Unknown: *Wassup sexy, how u been?*

I read the text, feeling confused. *Who the hell is this?* I wonder. I don't respond thinking surely they have the wrong number. Only one person should be texting me some shit like that. I leave my phone on the coffee table.

I dress in a pink and black Niké sweatsuit, pink and black Dunks, and put my hair up in a messy bun. I pull the zipper of my zip-up hoodie down a little to make sure the 'S' shows on my chain full of diamonds, a birthday gift from Shine last year. She has a matching chain with an 'N' on it. *Relationship goals, I know.* I put small round diamond earrings in my ears and a little mascara on for finishing touches. Less is more sometimes. I decide I want to take a cute selfie and send it to Shine before I head out, so I go back to the living room to grab my phone.

My touchscreen shows 2 unread messages. I unlock my phone and open my messages.

Unknown: *Damn. No love for the kid no mo'? Dat's cold.*

Unknown: *So bitch u ignorin' me now? U gon' make a nigga pull up on you forreal.*

A bad feeling comes over me that I know who this is. Chills run through me as I try to think of what I should do. I should call Shine, but she might take it too far. She doesn't tolerate disrespect. At. All. I sit on the couch and try to gather my thoughts, feeling my anxiety heighten and my pulse going 90 to nothing.

Me: *LEAVE ME ALONE. I don't want any problems. I am happy now in my life, in my relationship. Lose my number.*

Immediately, he responds.

Unknown: *Ha! Happy? Bitch, u think I'ma let u play house wit dat hoe u runnin' 'round wit? U got me fucked up.*

Me: *I'm serious, Treyton. Leave. Me. Alone. If you know what's best for you, you will move on with your life.*

I sit there for fifteen minutes, staring at the screen. There is no response. A little relieved, but still pretty shaken up by hearing from Trey makes me think twice about being in public today. But maybe having Ari with me would have him hesitant of making a scene out in the open. He's always been a private person. Thankfully, the nail salon is across the street from Shine's barber shop. I'll be in her eyesight which makes me feel a little less unsafe.

As I drive to the salon, I can't help but check the rearview mirror every 20 seconds feeling like I might be being followed. I don't see anything unusual, but the feeling is too strong for me to shake it. *Nevaeh, stop trippin',* I tell myself. Taking deep breaths, I try to calm myself down as I pull into the parking lot of the salon. Ari's car - a sky blue Nissan Maxima - is in the space next to me. I hop out and walk with a purpose to the entrance, trying not to draw attention to myself.

"Bitch, you'll never guess who texted me," I don't even say hello to Ari before I update her on the latest disturbance. "Trey," I tell her before she can even ask who. "He is out of jail. I don't know how the hell he got my number, but he's already talking about pulling up on me, girl."

"WHAT?! Did you answer him? Did you tell Shine?" she asks with panic in her voice.

"I just told him to leave me alone. And hell no, I didn't tell Shine. She'd hunt him down before he could even get to me. But she's already seemed so stressed out lately... I don't wanna bother her with no shit like that."

"Maybe you should call the cops."

"That'll just make it worse. I can handle it. What's he gonna do? Beg for me to take his ass back like last time?" I rolled my eyes thinking about the last time I saw Trey, he was literally on his knees begging me to give him another chance.

"Or fucking kill you! That's the worst that could happen!"

"Don't be so dramatic, Ari. I don't even know why I'm worried about him. Let's just enjoy this day. I don't ever get to see you. I don't wanna spend this time talking about the past." She agrees, changing the subject to tell me how she's been lately and I am thankful for the distraction.

The rest of the day goes by smoothly. After our nails finally dry, Ari and I have lunch together at Olive Garden. Then we hit a few clothing stores filling the trunks of our cars with shopping bags. I buy a new black lingerie set from Victoria's Secret to wear for Shine when we get some extra time to spend together. Ari makes me promise to spend time with her more often before we decide to call it a day.

"Don't be such a stranger, Vae. You're my best friend. I know you're happy and busy as hell, but I don't like not hearing from you. Especially now that we know Trey is out," she looks at me with so much worry that my eyes water a little. Blinking the tears away, I hug her tightly.

"I'm not going anywhere. I'll always be your sister, you know that. I will be intentional from now on. I promise," I tell her. She seems to accept that and walks over to her car, unlocking it from the button on her key ring. We both pull off at the same time, turning onto the road in opposite directions. Once again, I am alone. I use my Bluetooth to connect my car's speaker to my phone and call Shine.

She picks up on the first ring, like always. "Aye, ma."

"Hey, baby. I'm on my way home. I spent the whole day with Ari."

"How'd that go?"

"Good," I say. "We got our nails done, had lunch at Olive Garden, and spent a lot of money," I laugh a little.

"You deserved a day with your friend, baby. I'll be home soon, so I'll pick up something for dinner. I'ma cater to you tonight," her voice has me blushing and my clit throbbing.

"Sounds perfect. I love you. See you when you get home."

"See you then. I love you, too."

When I pull into the apartment complex, I waste no time getting inside. I lock the door immediately and make sure all the blinds are closed. Until Shine gets home, I'll be on high alert. I don't know how long Trey will wait to make his presence known, but I won't fall for his games. I know that much.

Chapter 7

Shine

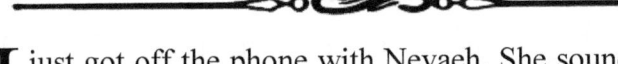

I just got off the phone with Nevaeh. She sounded a little stressed, which I thought a day with her friend would have helped with that, but I guess not as much as I'd hoped. I pull into the Taco Bell drive-through. I'm the third car in line, so I pull out my phone and see what's up on social media - nothing really, besides the same old shit that's always on my news-feed.

I go to Nevaeh's Instagram profile, scrolling through her posts. She's so beautiful. We have a doctor's appointment coming up to see if she's pregnant. I really hope there is a baby growing in there that would make our life even better than it already is. I try to picture myself holding a new born baby, a boy I hope, but either way I'm happy. A healthy baby is all we can ask for. I notice a new follower that seems to have recently liked her last post. I scroll through her page again, and recognize '@t_money' liked every one of her posts.

I click to go to the user's Instagram page and see who the hell is liking on my woman - the page is *blank* . It must have been recently created. There's no name or photo to show who the page belongs to, no posts, nothing. I wanna look into it more, but the cars ahead of me are moving forward, so I pull up to the speaker to place my order. I think back to the new Insta-user, maybe it's nothing, but I make a mental note to look deeper into it later on.

I pull up to the pick-up window and pay for our food, telling the cashier to keep the change. She passes the food and drinks to me, batting her eyelashes trying to get me to notice her. I take the food and put it in the passenger seat, driving off without a second look at the cashier.

By the time I get home and enter our apartment, Nevaeh is asleep on the couch covered up with the red, king-size comforter from our bed. I try to be quiet, stepping out of my shoes, leaving them by the door before I make my way to the kitchen table to set our food down.

I go to our bathroom to take a quick shower and step into some black Polo boxers and a matching Polo sports bra. Now that I'm comfortable, I go back to the kitchen to heat our food up. I bring our food to the living room and put it on the coffee table, lifting Nevaeh's legs up and sliding up under her. She wakes up slowly, and as if she just realizes she was asleep, she jumps up and looks at me like she's seen a ghost.

"Baby, it's me," I put my hand on her shoulder so she'll calm down. "You're covered in sweat. You feel OK?"

"Must've just been a bad dream. I- I'm okay. I didn't realize I fell asleep," she looks me up and down. "How long have you been home?"

"Less than an hour. I took a shower 'cause I didn't wanna get no hair on anything from the client's I had today. I stopped at Taco Bell I know that's your favorite," I say, reaching over to grab the plate I put her soft tacos on. "And I remembered to grab you a fork, 'cause you know you're the only person I know that uses a fork to eat tacos. Ol' boujee ass," we laugh together and she can't even say anything back to that.

We eat together. We talk a little, but she seems unusually quiet and short with her responses. She's not her normally bubbly self. I'm not sure what's up, but if something was going on I know she'd tell me, so I blame it on her hormones changing.

I bring the dirty dishes to the kitchen sink once we finish eating, rinse them, and put them in the dishwasher. I make my way back to the couch and put my phone next to hers on the coffee table before fitting myself behind Nevaeh under the comforter. She turns to face me, nuzzling her face against my chest and I wrap my arms around her. She falls back asleep within seconds. I kiss her forehead and doze off too.

***

I am woken up by one of our phones going off, alerting that a text came through. I try to ignore it, whoever it is can wait til the morning. The clock on the wall is hard to read in the dark, but when I squint I can tell the hands of the clock show that it's 3 in the morning. The phone alerts again, *another* text. I open my eyes again, looking towards the coffee table and noticing the screen of Vae's phone is lit up. *Who is texting her at 3 in the fuckin' morning?* My thoughts start to go off the deep end.

I reach over her and grab the phone. Both texts are from an unknown number, but I have to read the second message three times to make sure my eyes ain't playing tricks on me.

Unknown: *When u gon' let me in dat pussy again?*

Once more, I read those words. I can't fucking believe this shit. I jump up and snatch Nevaeh up by her hair. "Bitch, who the fuck is this textin' you?" I drag her to the middle of the floor, jerking her around like a rag-doll with her hair wrapped around my hand.

"Shine! Shine, stop! You're hurting me!"

"Hurting you? Hoe, you got some explainin' to do!" I throw her against the wall and she falls to the floor.

"Bitch, get the fuck up," I say, walking towards her slowly. "I'm good to you. I treat you like a fuckin' queen and you out here fuckin' some nigga?" She tries to get up off of the floor, but I kick her in her side and she collapses again.

"Shine, please," she begs, not phasing me a bit with her tears.

"Shut the fuck up," I say, kicking her again. "You wanna fuck these niggas out here while I'm being loyal to yo' grimy ass," I pull her up by her hair again. "Fuck you."

"Shine, no!" I back-hand her hard enough for her ears to ring. Blood immediately starts running from her mouth and she puts her hand up to her mouth wiping the blood away. "Please," she cries again.

I wrap my hand around her throat, squeezing tight to cut off her oxygen. "Bitch, I could kill you right now." I choke her until her body starts to shake. When she stops fighting against me, I release her, watching her drop to the floor again. I walk to the door, unlock it, and open it wide. She tries to crawl to the hallway. Before she can get too far, I snatch her by the hair again and drag her to the open door.

"No! Shine, please let me explain. Please don't do this to me. Let me go!" She tries to loosen my grip from her hair with both hands.

I push her out the door. "I am letting you go, right out the door. Go lay up wit' that nigga you fuckin', 'cause you ain't staying in here no more." I slam the door in her face.

I let my anger get the best of me. I've never put my hands on her before. I loved her too much to ever hurt her. I can't believe she would cheat on me. I really showed her different. I ain't never put in all this effort into any other relationship the way I have with Nevaeh. I've been in love once before, but the love I have with her is on another level. She just fucked that up.

I never wanna see her face again...

I feel that way now, but I don't know how long I can be away from her. *How could she do this to me? How can I ever trust her again? What do I not give her that she needs to go searching for somewhere else?* My thoughts are running wild.

"Shine!" Nevaeh screams my name like screaming my name like someone is trying to kill her. *That's how it should feel to lose me. Good.* I ignore her scream... until she screams again, this time even louder. It breaks my heart to hear her so broken.

I open the door. What I see stops me dead in my tracks. Nevaeh is holding her stomach, crying hysterically. There is a pool of blood on the ground... right between her legs.

"Take me to the hospital!"

I don't even have time to think. I pick her up, cradling her in my arms, and carry her to my car. I lay her across the backseat and jump into the driver's seat. I speed off towards the emergency room with Nevaeh crying out in pain behind me, and I pray that what's happening is not what I think it might be.

Chapter 8

one week later...

Lo

"Hello?"

"Aye, Lo. What's up wit' you?" I hear Shine's voice and realize how long it's been since I've heard it. I put on my left blinker before I pull into the Shell station, stopping at the gas pump to fill up the tank.

"What the hell, man?! Where you been? I ain't heard from you in over a week, thought you dropped off the face of the earth. What's up wit' you?" I ask with concern in my voice, putting my debit card in the payment slot of the gas pump. I don't hear her say anything for a minute or so " Shine, you good?"

"Vae was p- pregnant... she lost the baby. She just got out the hospital two days ago. It was my fault, Lo... I-"

"Wait, pregnant? So, the IVF thing y'all went through, it worked? And what you mean 'your fault'?"

"Yeah, it worked... and I mean it was *my* fault. I lost my shit on her. Bruh, I ain't never put my hands on her before. One of her ex's hit her up in the middle of the night and I lost it. She been home two days and won't even let me in the apartment. I been staying at a hotel," she says, which is hard to believe coming from her. I can hear the guilt in her voice. She usually doesn't show her emotions, so this shit is really bothering her. Shine and Nevaeh have a strong bond, I'd really hate to see that severed.

"Man, that's cold. Listen, she gon' come around. Y'all in love - the kinda love other people don't even wanna be around, because they wish they had it. So, just chill my nigga. Y'all gon' be good," I reassure her, hoping that I'm telling the truth. If Shine loses Nevaeh I'd hate to see the rage she lets out on anyone that steps in her path.

"Yeah, I hope you're right. You heard from Mookie?"

"Nah, I was 'bout to hit her up. Things seem to be 'laxed lately. That's probably a good thing though, because nobody will suspect what's brewing this way," I explain. "Let me pull up on her. I'll get at you later."

"Bet," is all Shine says before ending the call.

I finish at the pump and put the cap on my tank. Crazy how shit happens. Talking to Shine makes me think about my own dysfunctional ass relationship with Keisha. Ever since she tried to put me out of her apartment for not giving her enough of my time, we've been trying to work things out. I've been staying with her every night since then, fucking her real good, and giving her my undivided attention. When shit hits the fan, she'll be the perfect alibi, especially since she has no knowledge of our plans.

I get back into my truck and start the engine, then send Mookie a quick text to let her know I'm on my way to her place before hitting the road with my speakers blaring Lil Durk's song (featuring J. Cole), "All My Life".

All my life (all my life)

They been tryin' to keep me down

(They been tryna keep me down)

All this time (all this time)

Never thought I would make it out

(Never thought I'd make it out)

Listening to those words, I think about how much better things are gonna get once we secure this bag. Once we get this money, we'll invest it and watch it multiply. The streets raised us, but we gotta be better examples for these young niggas out here. We need to be raising the next generation to be leaders, instead of letting them fall victim to this corrupt ass legal system. Shaking my head, I let the music drown out my thoughts as I drive.

***

"So, when's the drop coming in?" I ask Mookie pointedly. She laces me up on all the info she's come up on since the last time we spoke. Keno been spilling all Rah Rah's secrets to Mookie. I listen to her with a smile on my face, nodding to let her know I hear her, while thinking to myself. *Loose lips sink ships. It's 'bout to be the Titanic in this bitch.*

"The delivery comes in on Friday at midnight - that's 6 weeks from now," Mookie informs me, scrolling through the notes on her iPhone double-checking the details. She made sure to get the correct day and time for the drop there's no room for error. "That Saturday night is the Fredo Bang concert at Bella Noche. Everybody will be there, so the streets will be quiet. Low activity is best."

"Right. Shine is talking care of weapons and whatever else we need. She has some shit goin' on right now, but I'll get wit' her and give her the update," I reach for my phone to check the time out of habit.

"OK. Keno also told me that Rah Rah doesn't let Ms. Kim stay in the house when the deliveries come in. He doesn't want her to be able to identify any faces if shit gets popped. So, he sends her on a 'mini-vacation' for the whole weekend," she looks away, seeming relieved that an innocent old lady won't be getting caught up in any crossfire.

"Good to know. Other than all that, you been good? I know things wit' you and him been rough," I look at her reading her facial expression, waiting for her response.

"Oh, I'm fine. You know me - ain't nothing stopping my happiness," she tries to sound convincing, but I don't buy it.

"Mmhmm." When she doesn't say anything else, I stand to let myself out. "Take care of yourself, Mook. You know we give a fuck about you. You need to give a fuck about yourself, too."

***

After a short drive to Keisha's apartment, I let myself in her door and go straight to the bathroom to hop in the shower. The water is hot and beating down on my back as I reach for the Old Spice body wash on the shower rack, squirting and lathering it on the washcloth. While washing my body, I hear a sound coming from somewhere in the house. Maybe I'm just paranoid, but I ain't taking any chances. I rinse off quickly, and turn off the water, stepping out of the shower to grab a towel and dry my body off. I wrap the towel around my hips and walk out of the bathroom, ready for whatever lies on the other side of the door.

Keisha's bedroom light is turned on and her door is wide open. She must have finally made it home.

"Bae?" I walk down the hallway towards her bedroom.

"In here, baby," she hollers and I'm relieved to hear her voice. "Traffic was already bad enough, so it didn't help at all that it started pourin' down raining out of nowhere!" She's in rare form tonight. I smile at her as she strips down to her bra and panties, leaving a trail of clothes behind her as she passes me to head towards the shower.

I grab her arm, pulling her into my arms. I kiss her deeply and I feel the tension leave her body as she parts her lips enough to let my tongue infiltrate her mouth. The only thing between us besides her underwear is the towel around my waist, a problem that could be solved quickly. Before things get too heated, I let her go and slap her on her ass as she makes her way to the bathroom. She knows exactly where to find me when she gets out the shower. I'm ready to put her pretty ass to sleep.

Chapter 9

two weeks later...
Shine

Reading that text message in Nevaeh's phone from her ex really put a burden on a nigga's heart. I even shed tears over that shit. I really love her more than anything, especially since I found a loyal woman that loves me unconditionally - flaws and all.

What hurt me the most was the fact that she knows my past and how I used to treat woman before I met her. After the last toxic relationship I was in, I made a promise to myself that I'd never put my hands on another woman again, especially one that I fall in love with. I had learned to talk out my problem, no matter how big it is, instead of resorting to physical abuse to express my hurt or anger.

Nevaeh and I had been planning a family. We were having a baby. I foolishly let my rage get in the way of that and cause her to lose our first child. The pain of that has been keeping me up at night, tossing and turning in my own grief and guilt.

Despite the fact that I've been catering to her every need, it still hurts me to even look in her eyes. At the emergency room, Nevaeh told the nurse that she had accidentally fallen. They did an ultrasound on her immediately and followed up with an MRI. Once the doctor told us the baby's heart was no longer beating, they did a procedure to remove the dead fetus from her uterus. They informed us that she had a broken rib and prescribed her pain medication for the discomfort that caused her.

I was still angry with her, but I didn't wanna leave her side. The doctor eventually came in to tell us that they would keep her for a few days for observation. When visiting hours ended, I returned to our apartment and found her phone to read the rest of the messages. I soon realized how bad I fucked up, because she was straight dissin' that nigga, Trey - her ex from years ago who had just gotten out of jail. I should have known that she would have put any nigga in their place that stepped to her wrong.

After a whole week of making me sleep in a hotel bed, she finally let me come back home. That was progress. We did talk about trying the IVF transfer again once she heals completely. As for tonight though, I plan on making love to my queen. I really can't cook, but for her I'd move mountains, so I'm up for it. When we first met, I thought she was a salad girl, but nah, that's out of the question. So, I'm whipping up some fried pork chops and some seasoned French fries to go with it.

Whatever it takes for her to let that guard down she put up; I'll even eat her booty if she'll let me. She won't even let me touch her right now, trying to play stubborn but I know she likes her pussy ate more than anything, so I'm going with my move tonight. If she tries to play hard, I'm just gonna spread them legs open and dive in. *She knows damn well dat pussy is mine,* I think to myself.

I fix my baby a plate of food and grab her a Root Beer out of the fridge. As I head upstairs, I hear the sound of the TV coming from our bedroom letting me know she's probably awake now. I ease into our bedroom and notice that she's watching *Love and Hip Hop: Miami.* That's our favorite show, so we don't miss a Monday, no exceptions.

I walk towards her, plate of food in my hand, and she gives me the meanest mug she's ever given me. I try to hold in my smile but can't help myself. She looks hesitantly at the food; I assume she's trying to decide if she will take it or not, but I know her mean ass is hungry. I sit the plate and soda on the nightstand and walk to the bathroom to take a shower. I want to give her some space, but as I step into the shower my mind is racing a hundred miles per hour hoping she accepts my kind gesture as an opening for us to talk.

Yeah, she let me come back home, but still she has not let me come back to our California king and I'm not feeling sleeping on that damn couch another night. A nigga back is sore and stiff as a muthafucka, so that shit is dead tonight.

If the cooked meal don't cut it, I'm going with Plan B - eating that booty... straight the fuck up.

After a 30 minute shower, I hop out and dry off, putting on my red Polo boxers, red Polo sports bra, and a white muscle shirt. Entering the bedroom again, I notice Nevaeh has eaten the food - that's a plus. "Can I watch TV with you, baby?" I ask her, sitting on the bed.

"No."

Fuck that, I think. *This is my shit.* I grab a pillow from the head of the bed and lie down at the foot of the bed. I know she's hurting and grieving, but enough is enough with the silent treatment. I start waving my foot around in her face, blocking her view of the TV.

"Stop before I knock you off this bed!" She laughs a little, but still has the mean ass look on her face, stubborn ass woman.

"You ain't gon' do shit. Please talk to me, Vae," I say slowly moving closer to her.

"I'll talk when I feel like it. Now is not the time, so just leave me the fuck alone."

"Girl, please," I ignore her attitude and crawl to the top of the bed next to her. Before I know it she pushes me right off the bed. I look up at her in shock but get off the floor with a quickness and snatch the comforter right off of her, yanking her little ass towards the edge of the bed.

"It's been three weeks since I taste this pussy. Shit, I ain't even seen it. I'm gettin' some tonight," I tell her with my hands on her waist.

"Get off me!" She tries to push me away, but I ain't going anywhere.

"Stop actin' bad, like you don't want it, too. I know dat pussy is soaking wet just thinkin' 'bout it." She looks sexy as hell right now with her red boy-shorts and Niké bra on. How could she think I wasn't gonna get her dressed like this.

I pull her boy-shorts down and toss them to the floor. As I start kissing her inner thigh she tries to push my head away, but I don't hear her protesting, so I'm not stopping. I keep kissing, leaving a trail of kisses down her thigh, until I reach her honeypot. She is so wet, just as I thought, so I latch on to her clit and start to suck while rotating my tongue like my life depends on it. I slide two fingers into her and she moans for me. I love the sound of that. Still working on her clit with my tongue, I start working my fingers in and out of her at a fast pace - like I'm bustin' her up with my strap.

"Fuck! Don't stop," she begs me loudly. I am definitely finishing this meal since I haven't ate yet tonight. I keep sucking and kissing her pussy til her legs are shaking and she tries pushing my head away again. I'm not giving up.

Her juices cover my chin and lips as I come up to look at her with a smirk on my face. She looks back at me with lazy eyes but she does not move an inch, so I crawl on top of her. When I kiss her softly, to my surprise, she kisses me back.

I pull my face back and look at her again. "Nevaeh, I love you. I'm so sorry for everything that happened," I confess.

She starts crying and I gently kiss her tears away, moving towards the foot of the bed again to stand over her. I give her a smile that says I'm up to something and she returns a look that says she believes I'm crazy. She's probably right.

With no warning, I grab her ankles and turn her over on her stomach. "Get on your knees and arch your back," I order and she submits to my demand without hesitation. "Stay still."

She does as she's told, but not for long as I spread her ass cheeks and start circling my tongue around her hole. She looks back at me to see if she's trippin' or not, but loses herself in the moment once again when I stick my tongue in her ass and start moving in and out of her, my fingers playing with her clit simultaneously. Her moans fill the room and it's all the motivation I need to turn things up a notch.

I slide two fingers inside her pussy, still stimulating her clit with my thumb. "Shine, I- I'm cummin'... Baby-" She can no longer speak as I stop eating her ass to catch the sweet honey that's flowing out of her pussy. In the middle of her climax, I suck on her clit from behind and send her into another climax. She screams my name as I clean up the mess I made of her with my tongue.

Once she catches her breath, she turns over slowly to look up at me, surprise is all over her face. All I can do is laugh and her cheeks turn red as she blushes.

"I bet you ain't think a nigga was gon' eat dat ass, huh?" I question her jokingly, but I'm serious too. She smiles at me and my heart starts beating faster at the sight of it. I crawl in bed with her and pull the covers over us. "I'm willing to do whatever you need me to do to make us work. I really am sorry, baby. I can't imagine my life without you in it," I say to her, my voice is hardly louder than a whisper. I kiss the top of her head and tell her I love her.

"I love you more," she whispers back to me before drifting off to sleep in my arms, right where she belongs. Chills go down my spine. She didn't say *too,* She said *more...* and I know it's true. It is her love for me that allows her to forgive me when I don't deserve it, and I don't want to ever take that for granted.

I grab the remote from the nightstand and turn the TV on to the Celtics game. *That nigga Jaylen Brown is gon' be the next Michael Jordan,* I think to myself. Minutes later, my phone vibrates against the nightstand. Unlocking my phone, I read a text message from Lo.

Lo: *Basketball tomorrow? Zion City, the gym. Got that info we needed.*

I shoot him a text back to let him know I'll be there. I pull my girl closer to me, and as soon as my head hits the pillow it's lights out.

Chapter 10

Keisha

This nigga, Lo, is trying to be a lover-boy all of a sudden, but it's just too little too late. He took me to play with and it wasn't until I was ready to throw his ass out that he *tried* to get his shit together. We all know there's nothing more dangerous than a woman scorned. I *hate* him. Of course I haven't shown him that. He has no idea that I know all of his secrets. You know what they say: *All that is done in the dark will eventually come to the light.* That's facts.

Right after our big fight regarding all the distance between us, I tried to forgive him and let him back in. Not even a week later, I wasn't surprised when I checked his phone and found text messages that proved he was still cheating.

Nothing had changed. The joke was on me, but I guarantee I'll be the one having the last fucking laugh. So, I will play my position and continue to act as if I know nothing. I'll be the loving and understanding girlfriend for a little while longer, and once the tables turn, we'll see just how loving and understanding he's willing to be in return.

First, I have some important news to tell him. I'm pregnant. I hope Lo is ready to be a daddy, because I have a feeling this baby is gonna give him hell. I reach for my phone and call him as I leave out of the doctor's office.

"Wassup, sexy?" he answers on the first ring.

"Are you busy?" I put the key in the ignition of my royal blue Chevy Malibu, waiting for him to respond before I crank up and pull out of the parking space.

"Nah, what you need?" He sounds busy. Actually, he sounds like he's been running a marathon and can't catch his breath.

"Just come home. We need to talk. It's important," I respond impatiently.

"On my way, baby."

"OK." My sick mind kicks in and I wonder if he's fucking some bitch while he's calling me baby.

"Ke," he interrupts my thoughts, "I love you."

"Yeah, love you, too. See you at home," I say before hanging up the phone. I know I have to be better at pretending everything is great when it isn't even good. Maybe the news that we have a baby on the way will lighten up the vibe between us.

Once I finally make it home, I walk in the door and sit on the couch to wait for Lo. I'm a little anxious to see how he will react. It's not something we were planning for. But it will damn sure earn me a lot of his attention. Oh well if I can't stand his ass, I can still let him spoil me and worship the ground I walk on. No harm, no foul.

I hear Lo fumble with his keys before opening the door to the apartment and strolling in without a care in the world. He notices me and smiles looking as if he's completely innocent. He closes the door behind him, locking it, and walks over to me kissing my lips before sitting next to me.

"What we need to talk about that you couldn't tell me over the phone?" he asks, only now starting to look like he might be worried.

I pull out the positive pregnancy test and hand it to him. He looks down at it unsure of what the two blue lines mean.

"What is this? What does this mean?" he asks, sounding a bit panicked.

"I'm pregnant. It means we're having a baby," I explain to him as he stands up and paces the living room. He doesn't say a word for a few minutes. He doesn't even look at me. "So, you mad?"

"No."

"Well, what are you? 'Cause you're walking back and forth looking crazy." I cross my arms over my chest and look at him with one eyebrow lifted, waiting for his response.

"I just need a fuckin' minute, OK? Damn," he raises his voice slightly. He storms off to the bathroom, and not too long after the door slams shut I hear the shower running.

The nerve of this nigga to be fucking me raw every night and be mad that I'm pregnant. *What the hell did he think was gonna happen?* I stomp through the apartment towards the bedroom and slam the door behind me. Petty, I know, but he's not the only one mad right now. I collapse on the bed, exhausted from the bullshit, and before I know it I drift off to sleep.

I become alert when I feel Lo kissing my forehead, my nose, and then my lips. I open my eyes slowly and he's looking down at me.

"I'm sorry," he says, "I ain't mad that you're pregnant. I just don't know if I'm ready to be a father. Are you sure that you're pregnant? You know those store bought tests sometimes ain't accurate."

"I took that test a week ago. I had a doctor's appointment today and they just confirmed what I already knew," I explain. "I didn't tell you when I took the test, because I wasn't sure how you were gonna react and I wanted to be sure."

"Nah, I'm happy, babe. We gon' be good. Don't worry, I got you and this baby," he comforts me in the only way he knows how, kissing my lips again.

I turn away from him hoping to easily fall back to sleep. He pulls me into his body and once his breathing is steady, I know he's asleep. I put my hand on my stomach wondering if the baby can feel me yet, and join Lo in the land of dreams - the only place we'll have a *happily ever after.*

Chapter 11

Nevaeh

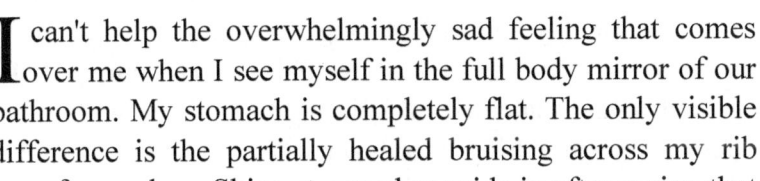

I can't help the overwhelmingly sad feeling that comes over me when I see myself in the full body mirror of our bathroom. My stomach is completely flat. The only visible difference is the partially healed bruising across my rib cage from where Shine stomped my side in after seeing that text from Trey. What's not visible is the fact that our baby is no longer growing inside of me.

I've experienced loss in my life, but this loss is on a higher level. I keep envisioning what our baby would have looked like. What was the gender? What would have been his or her first word? How many pounds would the baby have weighed at birth? So many questions and "what ifs" run through my mind, but those things will not come to pass, because the life of our first child ended... before it even really began.

I know there is a lot of healing left to do for both Shine and myself, but I also can't imagine leaving her. I know I am not the only one affected by losing our child it weighs heavily on her conscious as well. She tosses and turns throughout the night and has been unknowingly talking in her sleep as if our dead child visits her in her dreams. It's been difficult for us to comfort each other, but we are managing.

We've discussed a second embryo transfer and even went as far as scheduling an appointment at the fertility clinic. That appointment is in three weeks - the earliest we could get it scheduled after the miscarriage - and by then hopefully things will have become a little more like normal.

I walk out of my bathroom, through the bedroom, and find my way to the kitchen to brew some coffee before getting ready for the day ahead. Working from home has it's perks some days, because I'm comfortable in my purple Niké sports bra and matching athletic tights, and I don't have to change into anything more suitable for the workplace. Making my way to the living room coffee table, I open up my Mac Book Pro and clock into work while putting my Air-Pods in my ears to take incoming calls from customers. I check my work email account and respond back to majority of those before returning the kitchen to see that the coffee has finally finished brewing.

After retrieving my coffee mug from the dish washer, I fill my mug with dark roasted Community coffee and add two tablespoons of caramel creamer and three tablespoons of sugar. I have a lot to get done, so I need my coffee to be a little extra today. I taste test it to make sure it makes my taste buds happy, burning the tip of my tongue in the process. Satisfied with the taste, I walk back to the living room and make myself comfortable on the sofa.

I check my phone while I wait on a customer to call in for assistance with their insurance needs. There is a message from Shine saying she has plans to meet Lo tonight at the gym in Zion City. I send her a quick response telling her to be safe and that I love her, then check my Facebook to see if there's anything new happening in the world. I notice I have a DM from Mya, I haven't heard from her in a while, so I click on the message to read it fully.

Mya: *Biiiiiitchhh! I miss you! You never hit me up no more, what's that about? You too in love to make time for a real bitch or sum'?*

I shake my head at Mya's message. She's always been the same, wanting all the attention and will let you know in a heartbeat when she's feeling some type of way. I guess that's why we clicked when we first met. She sort of had me in the right place at the right time to meet Shine, so I feel a bit indebted to her I'll never tell her ass that, because she'd surely use it against me. I do need to be better about checking in on her though.

Me: *Girl, stop with the antics! You know if you need me I'm here - you wanna hang out when I get off work this evening?*

Mya: *Um, is that a trick question? OF COURSE!*

Me: *LOL, I get off at 5 - meet me at Chili's at 6.*

Mya: *Bitch, don't stand me up!*

I don't even respond to that last message, because she knows better. We may not always be in touch, but Mya has known me long enough to know my word is solid. I can't lie - I really look forward to having a girls' night out, because I haven't been out since my miscarriage. I've been in and out of depression, holding myself together when Shine is home and falling apart when she isn't present. I don't want to keep living like this. I want to move forward, but I feel so heavy. Maybe a night out, a few drinks, and a lot of laughter will do me some good.

Work goes smoothly for the rest of the day. I got a few breaks in between to finish up on two major papers that were due in my college courses and was able to schedule an appointment to get a manicure and pedicure at the end of the week. I decide to clock out of work about 30 minutes early, so I have time to clean up the apartment some before I meet Mya. Cleaning up doesn't take up too much time, so I take a quick shower and dress in some stone-washed jeans and a white Polo v-neck T-shirt with matching white Ugg boots. I grab my jean jacket, my phone, and my car keys before heading out the door.

***

I arrive at Chili's about five minutes before 6 o'clock, and of course Mya is already seated and waiting for me. She stands when she sees me with a big ass smile on her face. Before I can protest, she rushes to me and picks me up, spinning me around in circles.

"Put me down!" I yell at her playfully.

"Ugh. Fine. I just miss the hell outta you! I ordered our drinks already. You mind?" I know she is being polite by asking, because it doesn't make a difference to her whether I mind or not. I just shake my head and have a seat in the booth across from her, taking in the scenery of the restaurant.

Right on cue, the waitress approaches our table with our drinks. She is a Hispanic woman, probably not older than 30, with long, black, wavy hair, and there are worry lines on her forehead as if she carries more than just meals on her plate. I smile at her as she sets the drinks on our table. "Two Henney-ritas. Do the two of you need more time or are you ready to order?" she asks shyly. She takes her notepad out of the front pocket of her apron and clicks the end of her ink pen.

"Maybe just tortilla chips and salsa for right now," I respond. I don't have much of an appetite for food as of late, and nothing on the menu seems to change that.

"Bitch, please. You ain't gotta be boujee everywhere you go, sis," Mya rolls her eyes at me before to the waitress, "Ma'am, I'll have an order of mozzarella sticks, an order of sliders, and two orders of riblets in to-go boxes, please. I gotta feed my man, too." She looks at me again, narrowing her eyes as if I have committed the ultimate sin. The waitress repeats the order back to us to make sure she hasn't missed anything and leaves us without another word.

"What?! I don't have an appetite, but I'm here with you! Give me a break," I whine with my arms folded over my chest.

"Well, what the hell's been going on with you then?"

"I had a miscarriage," I don't look her in the eyes when I say it, because I don't want to let the tears fall. "Shine and I went through the IVF process and it worked for us, but I lost the baby. It's been really hard for us to move past it, especially me."

"Oh, shit. I'm so sorry to hear that. Are y'all gonna try again?"

"Yeah, we have an appointment scheduled in three weeks," I tell her before sipping the Henney-rita from the glass and putting it back on the table.

"That's good. How are things between you two since you lost the baby? Is the vibe awkward?" she inquires while drinking her own drink, not sipping but damn near gulping it down as if it's the last glass of water in the middle of the Sahara desert.

"Not really awkward - it's just that I've been depressed, so Shine never really knows what to say to comfort me, you know? She tries, but I just shut down. I don't want to shut her out, but I've never experienced anything like this before. I do want us to move forward, and I want my mind and body to be fully healthy for the next baby." I look away from Mya because my eyes are beginning to water. I blink the tears away and when I look back at her she is teary-eyed too.

"Got me all emotional and shit," she picks up a napkin and pats around her eyes to soak up the wetness. "You know I don't get all sentimental, but my heart really goes out to you and Shine. Life sucks sometimes, but if any two people could get through shit like this, it's the two of you," she says as she reaches for my hand and squeezes it in hers.

"Yeah, I agree. I believe we'll get through it. I just gotta pull myself together." I notice the waitress coming our way with the food we ordered. Once she gets to our table, she politely sets the food down and leaves after telling us she'll be back to check in on us soon.

"And somebody got a muthafuckin' birthday comin' up!" Mya exclaims, raising her voice a little and twerking her fat ass which brings eyes from all around the restaurant our way and embarrasses me. It wouldn't be her if she didn't draw attention everywhere she went. I just know my whole face is bright pink.

"Girl, who reminded you?!" I cover my face with both hands laughing at the scene she is making. "Lower your voice and sit your ass down while people are trying to enjoy their meals!"

"Who cares! We gon' turn the fuck up for sure. It's time to celebrate you, bitch! Put some color back into your life instead of that gray ass aura you been carryin' around." She digs into her food and doesn't even notice that my jaw drops at her words.

I can't even say anything, because she's right. It's time to get out of this funk. I'm not sure why Mya was so insistent that we spend time together but I am glad we did, because I realize that I can not allow this pain to consume me and stop me from living the life I have left to live.

We continue to talk about my upcoming birthday, our relationships, and what we've been up to since the last time we saw each other. For the rest of the night the vibe is happy and positive. We eat, drink, laugh, and carry on as if no one else is in the restaurant until the waitress comes over to give us the bill and informs us that the doors will be closing soon. Mya doesn't even allow me to split the bill with her, calling it an early birthday treat. We collect our belongings and she doesn't forget to grab her to-go boxes before we walk out the exit together hand in hand.

"I love you, sis. Keep your head up. Shit will get better," she says as she pulls me into her and hugs me.

"Love you, too. Thanks for reaching out. I really needed this tonight. I'll see you soon, right?"

"Duh! And if you need me, just call, OK? Don't be such a stranger," she pushes me in a playful way and walks in the direction of her charcoal gray Nissan Maxima that's parked a few spaces away from my car.

"I will, I promise!" I assure her as I sit in the driver's seat of my car and shut the door. I'm missing my woman so bad right about now, so I say a small prayer that she will make it home around the same time I will. We have a lot of making up to do. I pull out of Chili's parking lot in the direction of home, as H.E.R.'s song, "Every Kind of Way," flows through my speakers.

I wanna love you in every kind of way

I wanna please you no matter how long it takes

If the world should end tomorrow

And we only have today

I'm gonna love you in every kind of way

Chapter 12

Shine

"So, let me get this straight. Six weeks from now they make the drop Friday night - well, really Saturday at midnight. We move in during the Fredo Bang concert Saturday night. Mookie will be waiting at the back door to let us in and by that point she'll have the security system disabled. We hem them niggas up at gun point, get the code to the safe, get them for everything they got, and be out the door leaving no witnesses behind. Correct?" I ask while dribbling the ball down the basketball court and shooting it straight in from the free-throw line.

"Correct. And Mook said Ms. Kim is sent away on weekends that there's a drop so she'll be outta the way." Lo gets the lay-up and dunks the ball over my head laughing. I push him out the way and retrieve the ball, dribbling towards the net on the other side of the court as he picks himself up off the court and tries to catch up with me. "Damn, it's like dat?" he asks, his face in shock.

"Catch up, old man," I joke back with him, as the ball swishes into the net again.

"Fuck you, nigga."

"Let me find out old age is makin' you soft, bitch," I taunt him, laughing loudly. Lo reaches for me with a quickness, knocking the ball out of my hand and shooting from half-court. The ball goes right in.

"Nah, not at all youngin'. I never miss my target." Lo walks over to the bleachers as the ball continues to bounce and then roll in the opposite direction. I walk over to the bleachers as well and sit next to him. We don't say anything for a while, just looking off into the distance, deep in thought.

"We got this shit down to a science then. There's no room for error. I got the weapons and shit ready and I'll pick a rental car up that Friday," I say, breaking the silence. "I am planning Vae's birthday party for that Saturday night at Bella Noche. That'll be our alibi. We can dip in and out without much notice, and enough people will be able to attest that we were at the club if need be."

"Bet." He doesn't say anything else and still has this melancholy look on his face so I know something is up other than hittin' this lick.

"Man, what's your problem? Sum' happen since we last spoke?"

"It ain't a big deal."

"Shit, I can't tell. It's big enough for you to be in your chest behind it. You gotta be in a clear head space for shit to go right when it's time to take care of business. So, what the hell is up?" I ask, pressing him.

"Keisha is fuckin' pregnant." He puts his head down, shaking it in frustration.

"What's wrong wit' that?"

"I... I didn't think I could, you know... have kids."

"Why not?"

"I got a low sperm count," he says so quietly that I don't think I hear him correctly.

"You got what?"

"A low sperm count," he repeats in a louder volume.

I am surprised to hear him say that. Lo has always been a private person. He walks around looking so serious most of the time that it's obvious there's always a lot on his mind. You never really know what a person is going through though, even after knowing someone as long as I've known him.

"When did you find out you might not be able to have kids?"

"When I was a lot younger. I had to be fifteen or sixteen. Some shit went down with my mama and her ex-boyfriend.

They had a big ass fight and he was a big buff nigga, so I tried to defend her. She didn't do the same for me when he caught me later that night in the shower and raped me." Lo gets quiet for a second, trying to collect himself. I don't know what to say, so I remain quiet.

"I told my mama the next day," he continues. "She was mortified. She rushed me to the hospital and told the emergency room nurses that I had been raped. They did a rape kit and the damage was so severe that I was told it was likely I would never be able to father a child, that the chances we almost nonexistent. My mom concocted a story that she had let me go to a party with friends and I was intoxicated when I called her and told her I had been raped."

"Damn, Lo. That's fucked up." I say, finally finding words, but knowing that it doesn't make his circumstances any better.

"Yeah, she kicked me out afterwards. She said if I had been nicer to him then he wouldn't have had to teach me a lesson. I thought about going back to kill him, but she chose that bum ass nigga and she deserved to have that piece of shit in her life. I never went back. When he finally beat her ass until she couldn't take no more and left her without a dollar to her name, she hit me up and asked if she could stay with me 'til she got on her feet. I told her to never contact me again. That was the last time I heard from that bitch." He brushes the palm of his hand down his face and stands up, checking his watch.

"Damn. So, you think Keisha is pregnant by somebody else?" I questioned.

"That's what I'm thinking. But she ain't ever stepped out on a nigga before, so I don't know what to think, man. She's been dealin' with my shit for a long time, I'm thinking maybe I'm gettin' my karma," he walks to grab the basketball and put it in his gym bag.

"Karma is a bitch."

"Yeah. That bitch got Red Bottom stilettos on and is walking all over my fuckin' chest right now. I'm outta here, bruh. I'll holla at you later," he says, pulling the strap of his gym bag over his shoulder before walking off the court.

"A'ight," I say, heading out as well. I get to my car and think back on our conversation. I had no idea that shit went down when Lo was younger. It's a cruel fucking world out there. No mercy in these streets and even less in our childhood homes.

I put the car in reverse and back out into the streets, idling for a moment to send a text to my future wife letting her know that I'm on my way home. To my surprise she responds saying she's waiting for me patiently. I smile, because I know she is needing some of this good pussy I'm about to put in her life. I ain't trying to do the speed limit at all, because the faster I close this gap between us the better.

***

"Just as I thought," I say in her ear as I slide my fingers down her pussy lips and circle them around her hole, "you're so wet for me, ma." I wasted no time when I finally made it home and Nevaeh was sitting pretty on the couch watching TV, waiting for me. I got out of my clothes and positioned myself between her thighs. She was already naked, with nothing covering her body but the comforter from our bed that I tossed to the side so I could have complete access to her.

"Damn, baby, you missed me?" I slide my fingers in her pussy and her head falls back on the armrest of the couch as she moans quietly and spreads her legs wider for me.

"So much," she says in my ear as I slide my fingers back out and out them in her mouth. She sucks her honey off my fingers and I lean down to replace my fingers with my tongue, trying to reach the back of her throat. Still kissing her, I put her right leg over my shoulder and cross my right leg over her body to get in position so my clit lines up perfectly with hers. I slowly start to grind back and forth on top of her and start to suck and bite on her neck as she raises her hips to meet me.

"Mmm," she moans as I quicken my pace. I take her nipple between my thumb and index finger and squeeze gently. She starts bucking harder underneath me. "Ugh," she moans louder.

"You like that?" I ask, squeezing her nipple harder and rolling it between my fingers, grinding my clit hard and fast against hers. Our pussy juices crash against each other like waves against the ocean shore, the wetness of us dripping down to the cushions beneath us.

"Yes! Yes, baby. Don't stop," she answers, digging her nails into my back like she does when she's reaching her climax.

"Who dis pussy for?"

"You!"

Who's it for?" I ask again, grabbing a handful of her hair and tugging on it roughly.

"You, Shine, oh my- I'm about to cum!" As soon as she releases her juices, I join her and cum so hard I have to hold myself up so I don't collapse on top of her. I get off of her and sit back on the couch trying to catch my breath, while she does the same. I close my eyes and lean my head against the back of the couch, not even noticing that Nevaeh is moving until I feel her hands on my thighs, spreading them apart.

"Bae, what are you-"

"Shhh...," she interrupts my question and spreads my pussy lips before she latches on and starts sucking my clit. I don't even put up a fight. I let her do her thing and she does just that - licking and sucking my clit like it's a delicacy. When my toes curl and my eyes roll back, I grab her head and guide her, pushing my pussy into her mouth.

"Fuck, baby, it's right there," I say, bucking in her mouth harder before coming. She takes her time licking me clean and comes up with my wetness covering her lips and chin. "Come here," I demand and she does, curling up against me and I wrap my arms around her. There's no other place in the world I could think to want to be than right here, holding her.

Chapter 13

five weeks later...
Keno

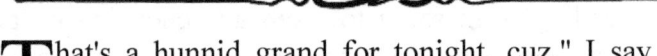

"T̶hat's a hunnid grand for tonight, cuz," I say in Rah Rah's direction, putting the last stack of bills in the black leather briefcase he provided.

"Better not be a penny short either or you won't be seein' the sunrise in the morning, nigga," Rah Rah answers with a cold stare as he walks into the room.

"I ain't ever came up short before, so why now?" I ask.

"Right, right," is his only response before grabbing the briefcase and heading towards the back door. "No funny shit while I'm gone. Don't make me regret my fuckin' decision." He lingers for a second at the door, looking around the trap house. Rah Rah is a light-skinned, 5'7", Park Town nigga. He was raised by the same streets he's running today. As the biggest drug supplier in B.R., he is known for being merciless and ruthless which is what led him to be the most feared and respected. "Tell Kim to clean up all these liquor bottles she got everywhere wit' her trifflin' ass," he slams the door behind him and I'm left to my own devices.

Rah Rah promoted me last week as his second in command. He pretty much raised me over all these years, so to have finally earned his trust ain't something I'm taking lightly. He's getting older, so I imagine he will want to retire out the game eventually and I'll be able to run this empire he created. *I just gotta get a grip on this fuckin' coke problem,* I think, while forming a line of powder on the coffee table in front of me and leaning over to snort it up my left nostril. The rush it gives me is like no other, but it'll surely be the death of me if I don't shake this shit soon.

My senses come alive and I move around the trap house swiftly, speeding from room to room and checking on all the aspects of our business operation. I start picking up the liquor bottles, because Ms. Kim is sprawled out on a loveseat in her room with the door wide open and the TV blaring. I close her door to give the old lady some privacy, though she's completely oblivious to anything going on around her at the moment.

Everything has been running smoothly lately. We are expecting a big delivery to come in next week, so I've had to check and double check inventory and move shit around in storage to make sure all is secured and in place for the drop. Nobody would suspect that this dead end trap is a multimillion dollar enterprise. *And one day, I'll run all this shit.* The hairs on the back of my neck stand with excitement.

It's been a couple days since I got my dick wet inside Mookie, so I send her a text telling her to be in here in 20 minutes or I'm putting more than good dick on her. She is terrified of me and I find that pleasing. The fear in her eyes when I'm fucking her gets me off even harder. I don't know what comes over me, but it's thrilling to hear her screaming my name - whether it's because I'm beatin' that pussy up or just beatin' her ass for the hell of it. I let my frustrations out on her in whatever way I please, and she takes it like the down bitch she is. While I wait for her to arrive, I finish counting up the last bit of cash we made tonight with a shit eating grin on my face, because life is almost too good to be true.

Chapter 14

Lo

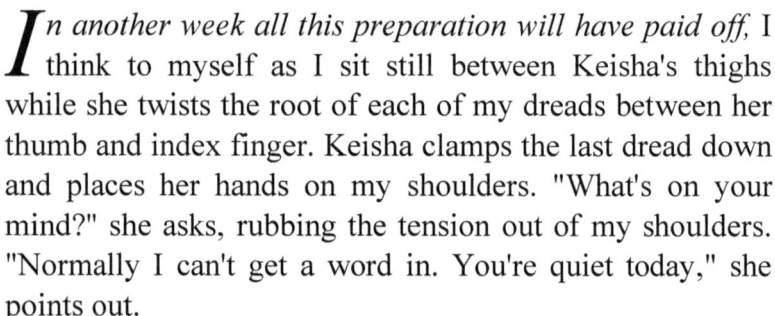

*I*n another week all this preparation will have paid off, I think to myself as I sit still between Keisha's thighs while she twists the root of each of my dreads between her thumb and index finger. Keisha clamps the last dread down and places her hands on my shoulders. "What's on your mind?" she asks, rubbing the tension out of my shoulders. "Normally I can't get a word in. You're quiet today," she points out.

"I'm good, bae. Just thinking 'bout the birthday party Shine's throwing for Nevaeh. You know if everything ain't on point Shine's gon' be on both our asses." I laugh it off.

"Don't I know it," she responds.

"So, I'm just checkin' shit off in my head to make sure I did all she asked me to do. The party gon' be lit." Just as soon as I stand and walk towards the kitchen, my phone starts going off on the kitchen counter. I notice Shines name before I answer. "You gon' live a long time, my nigga. Wassup?"

"We're headed to Nevaeh's parents' house. I wanted to all you though, 'cause the doctor from the IVF clinic called us this morning," she said, excitement obvious in her voice.

"What the doc say?"

"Vae is pregnant! Again... She's high-risk since she had a miscarriage not long ago, but they said all her blood work looks good. We go back in four weeks for another ultrasound," she explains, barely taking a breath between sentences.

"That's wassup. I'm happy for y'all, for real."

Keisha walks into the kitchen. "That's Shine? How they doin'?" I can tell by the look on her face she was ear hustlin' on the slick.

"The IVF transfer worked. Nevaeh's pregnant," I relay the good news to her.

"Put it on speaker!"

Pressing the speaker button, I put the phone down on the counter. "Shine, put your phone on speaker. You know Ke is extra," I tell her.

"It's on speaker," she confirms.

"Congratulations you two!" Keisha interjects before I can say another word. "We pregnant together, bitch! Sounds like some cute ass maternity pics," she laughs.

"Thank you, Ke," Nevaeh says. "We'll link up for the pics for sure. You'll be at my birthday party, huh?"

"Duh, I'll be there! We'll be the only two sober bitches, so you know we gon' have to look after everybody else," Keisha answers her.

Nevaeh's laughs at that "Well, we'll see y'all soon then."

"That's a bet. Y'all have a safe trip. Shine, I'll holla at you later on, a'ight?" I say.

"A'ight. Later." she replies.

I press the red button on the touchscreen, ending the call. Keisha has already exited the kitchen, so I go to look for her, leaving my phone on the counter. When I find her, she's sitting on the edge of our queen-size bed in silence, with her forehead creased in deep thought. Seems like the tables have turned.

I walk into the bedroom closing the space between us. "Now what's in your mind?" I inquire.

"Shine and Nevaeh's seem like they're really happy," she says without making eye-contact with me.

"What you gettin' at?"

"We used to be like that," she mumbles.

"You're unhappy?" I ask her, not really understanding where this shit is coming from. "I ain't makin' you happy?"

"I don't know, Lo. I was happy with you. And I know you been tryin' to put more effort into our relationship," she says, dancing around the point she's trying to make. "Ever since I told you I was pregnant, you just been so... so-"

"So, what?" I interrupt her, losing my patience.

"Distant! Not physically, but emotionally. It's like you ain't here," she looks up at me.

"I *am* here. What you want me to do? I ain't the type of nigga that just pours my heart out and shit," I explain. "So, what?"

"I never know how you feel."

"Well, I feel tired. I feel like I want you to order some food while I smoke me a blunt. I *feel* like you talk to fuckin' much and make shit harder than it needs to be," I tell her, my tone laced with irritation.

She doesn't respond to me at first, just looks at me like I've lost my damn mind. "Fuck it," she finally blurts out. "I'm through wit' it." She gets up off the bed and bumps my shoulder as she walks past me and out the bedroom door.

I shrug my shoulders. *Hormones,* I think to myself, shaking my head back and forth in dismay. I walk out the door that leads to the terrace, taking a lighter out of the pocket of my hoodie to light my blunt. *I hope Keisha does order us some take-out, 'cause a nigga 'bout to have the munchies big time,* I think. I blow smoke rings into the air, looking up at the night sky.

Three stars and pale sliver of the moon is all I can make out behind the clouds that linger in the darkness. The only sound I hear is the chirping of crickets as I pull a couple more times from the blunt. I start to feel like I'm floating, so I make my way back into the bedroom, closing the door behind me. I strip out of my clothes and fall onto the bed. *Wild 'N Out* is playing on TV, so I watch that, laughing hysterically, until I am overcome by sleep.

Chapter 15

one week later...
Mookie

I hate that I'm missing Nevaeh's birthday party tonight, but I have to make sure things go according to plan. For that reason, I'm headed to Rah Rah's trap to meet Keno... for the last time. I know Shine and Lo planned to hit this lick mainly for a financial gain, but this shit is deeper than that for me. It's about *revenge.* I've been swallowing my pride, letting him do as he pleases, and turning a blind eye to his bullshit - all for the sake of keeping my enemy close. *Game point, nigga,* I think to myself, smiling at the images in my mind of what's about to go down while Cardi B's song, "Be Careful," blasts through the speakers of my car.

I gave you everything, what's mine is yours

I want you to live your life, of course

But I hope you get what you dyin' for

Be careful wit' me

I sing along to the words, really feeling the lyrics in the pit of my stomach. *That nigga shoulda been careful with me but he was careless instead, so his ass is fo' sho' 'bout to get what he's dyin' for,* I think. I put my silver Toyota Camry in park in Rah Rah's driveway and take my key out of the ignition. I sit in my car for a few minutes to collect myself, and send Lo a text to let him know I'm in position.

The sun is beginning to set, so I imagine everybody's getting prepared for Nevaeh's party. Everybody in the city's gonna show up for the Fredo Bang concert, so I know Bella Noche's about to be full to capacity. I wish I could be there, but there will be other birthdays and concerts. *A girl's gotta do what a girl's gotta do.* With that in mind, I exit my car and walk up the driveway, texting Keno to tell him I'm outside.

He opens the door as soon as I make it up the steps. "What's up, shawty?" he greets me. "You must be missin' yo' nigga or sum'," he smirks and opens the door wider to let me into the house.

"Rah Rah here?" I ask, looking around the trap to see if there's anything unusual going on.

"He in the basement. BJ is down there wit' him. We had that drop last night, so they been makin' sure everything's accounted for," he explains.

I nod my head. "I ain't seen BJ in a li'l minute. He came alone?" I inquire.

"Yeah."

"Well, are you too busy for me then since you got all this business to handle?" I whine and give him the most innocent look I can muster up.

"Nah," he says eagerly. "I'm good for the night. We can go to the back and chill, smoke, fuck, I'm wit' whateva you wit,' bae."

"Let me freshen up and I'll meet you back there," I tell him, biting my lip and winking at him flirtatiously before walking towards one of the guest bathrooms. I look to make sure he's headed the other way and change direction towards the security room. I know this house like the back of my hand. Keno's dumb ass never suspects a thing, always underestimating me, giving me too much information. Rah Rah would've killed him years ago if he only knew half the tea Keno has spilled.

I enter the security room, checking behind myself before closing the door. I have to be swift, because I know Keno will wonder what's taking me so long and come looking for me. I put the six digit password into the main computer and am granted access immediately. I freeze all of the security cameras, turn off all of the motion detectors, and disable all of the alarms. As fast as I went in, I exit the room, satisfied with my quick work. I text Lo to let him know that the system is down.

I walk towards the back of the house and find the room that Keno has made himself comfortable in. As I enter the room, I notice that he's completely naked, with the exception of his socks. His nine inch, thick, black dick is standing at attention and stops me dead in my tracks. He's using one hand to stroke his length, and the other to show me the he wants me to put my lips to use. *Get yourself together, bitch. One more time won't kill you,* I think as I approach him. I get on my knees between his legs, taking his dick into my mouth and he doesn't hesitate pushing himself down my throat. I pretend to be into it while I talk myself through the motions, *it'll all be over soon.*

Chapter 16

Nevaeh

Shine really went all out. Tonight has been *amazing*. We've been here for a couple of hours already and the energy hasn't begun to die down. I thought I might be a little jealous that everybody is drinking and feeling good, but I'm having so much fun that I'm not phased by it. This'll be the last big event I attend until the baby is born, so we have to make it count.

"Wassup, ma? You come here often?" Through all the noise, I could never mistake that voice. I smile as she puts her arms around my waist and pulls me against her.

"Sorry, I'm taken," I tease her. Shine picks me up and throws me over her shoulder, taking me by surprise.

"That mouth is gonna get yo' ass in trouble, ma," she taunts me.

"Shine! Put me down!" I laugh, hitting her shoulder playfully. I fight to get out of her arms like a toddler throwing a tantrum, but she doesn't budge.

When she finally puts me down, she presses the palm of her left hand against my stomach. "You fed our baby?"

"Of course. People been bringin' me plate after plate of food since we walked in the club, like I'm lookin' too skinny," I turn around and poke out my ass. "How's it look?"

She laughs. "They're just makin' sure you good, babe. You still fine. I ain't lyin'. You know I need somethin' I can grab on," she says, slapping me on my ass roughly.

"Mhmm, I know," I reply, blushing and biting my lip. "Did you see Keisha? She went to the restroom and never came back this way." I look around.

"Yeah, she's over there," Shine points to the left side of the stage. "Mya and Ari are with her. Go chill with your girls. I got somethin' I gotta do real quick. I'll see you in a few," she tells me, kissing my forehead before sending me on my way.

I move through the crowd towards my friends and take in the scene for about the hundredth time tonight. Bella Noche is the hottest club in B.R. The whole city is out showing love tonight. All the boss niggas at the bar are throwing shots back and checking out the view of the dance floor as asses are twerking and popping in every direction. All the tables are decorated with a centerpiece - an iridescent letter 'N' - to show that it's *my* night.

When I make it to Keisha, Mya, and Ari, they are in a tight circle discussing something that must be important. I place my hand on the dip of Keisha's back and she turns abruptly to see who is crazy enough to touch her. "What's up with the gossip circle?" I ask them. "Y'all look like y'all up to no good." Everyone's face looks guilty, but no one wants to speak first. I raise an eyebrow at them, waiting for an answer.

"Girl, ain't nothin' goin' on," Mya says finally, breaking the ice. "We just waiting for the show. You know Fredo Bang is a hot nigga. I'm tryna see what that dick like," she laughs.

"Bitch, he ain't even gon' notice yo' crazy ass!" Keisha teases her. "It's your night though, sis," she brings her attention back to me. "I'm just tryna make sure these two drunk hoes don't embarrass us," she looks at Mya and Ari, who are grinding on each other, and we both laugh. The crowd turns all the way up when Fredo comes to the stage to perform the first song on his set list, "Last One Left."

(Real one)

How many times I gotta prove myself?

Every promise that I told I kept

I'm one of the last ones left

The crowd sings along. I look around for Shine, but don't see her, so I enjoy the music and the time I get to spend with my girls. Keisha bucks me up to sing with her and we dance like we're in a music video, not caring who's watching. The song ends and changes to the next one on the set list, "Say Please."

Don't leave me lonely, yeah

I need you to stay by my side

Wit'chu I'm always satisfied

Without you like walkin' in the blind

I ain't tryna say my goodbyes

I'm just tryna make shit clear

Tell me what you want, what you wanna hear

Tell me what you need

Tell me do I gotta beg for it, I'm not scared to say please

I smile big and sing along thinking of Shine, because this is one of our songs. Keisha grabs my arms and pulls me closer to the stage. "Why we up here? I was good back there," I tell her, trying to walk back towards the table behind us.

"Just stand up here with me," she says. "You know your blind ass can't see from back there anyway," she jokes. I let her win the battle for now and enjoy the performance. At the end of the song, Fredo stops singing, but the instrumental continues to play. I notice him move to the side of the stage, away from the mic, and point to the right of the stage. My jaw drops when I see Shine walk onto the stage and approach the microphone, looking directly at me. She's dressed down in Polo attire from head to toe, her line is fresh even from here, and the diamonds in her ears, around her neck, and on her wrist sparkle as the stage lights hit them.

"Happy birthday to my queen, Nevaeh," she announces. Everyone looks at me. They are cheering and applauding, wishing me a happy birthday. I feel my face heat up and my cheeks are likely flushed pink from the unexpected attention. "I wanna thank everyone for comin' out. Give it up one good time for Fredo Bang!" Shine gestures towards him and I see him nod his head towards the crowd. "He ain't finished yet. But I took it upon myself to take a li'l intermission," she says, winking at me.

"Vae, we really been through it over the past few years. The highs have been heavenly, the lows been hell. I thought you would've given up on us by now, I wouldn't have blamed you, but you never left my side." My eyes are already watering. *Thank God I put on waterproof mascara,* I think. I blink away the tears that threaten to fall. The crowd is completely silent for the first time tonight. "We have much more good on the way," she looks down at my stomach, smiling. "But the hard times are gonna come at us even harder," she looks down at her feet as if she's a little nervous. "Can you come up here with me?" she asks.

I walk up the steps on the left of the stage with Lo at my side making sure my clumsy ass don't trip and fall. I hold my head high as I walk towards her. "I'm here," I say shyly.

"You're here," she reiterates, "right by my side." She reaches into her pocket and takes out a little black velvet box. "And I wanna know if you wouldn't mind staying there for the rest of our life?" She gets down on one knee in front of me, opening the box to reveal the most beautiful diamond ring I've ever seen. I cover my face with both hands, giving myself time to gather my emotions.

I look down at her, the music still playing in the background. "Yes! Yes, yes, yes," I drop to my knee in front of her, so we are eye level and out my arms around her neck.

"I love you, Vae," Shine says in my ear.

"I love you more." She stands and pulls me to my feet as well. "She said 'yes,'" she announces into the microphone. Everyone is already cheering and clapping for us before she gets the word out. *Who knew tonight was gonna turn out like this,* I think. Shine takes the ring out of the box and places it on my left ring finger. She grabs me by my waist, escorting me off of the stage, as Fredo makes his way back to the mic and the track changes once again.

"You probably wanna have more girl time now with your friends, right? Before we head out?" Shine asks.

"Yeah, baby," I answer her. "Not too much longer. Just gotta show off a li'l," I smile and hold my left hand up in the light to see the big princess-cut diamond that's encased in smaller diamonds. Shine grabs my left hand and kisses the ring. She pulls me closer to her. "I'm gon' kiss on somethin' else later," she whispers, sending a tingling sensation down to my clit.

I'm blushing again. "Whenever you ready," I tell her, biting my lip. "See you in a few." I spot my friends and walk their way. Ari notices me first and tells the other two, so they all turn and walk to meet me.

"Let us see it, bitch," Mya says, extra as hell like always. "Daaammmmn, that bitch is fire! She went to Jared, huh?" Mya takes my hand in hers and brings the ring into the light. "Yeah, she definitely went to Jared."

I snatch my hand from hers. "Bitch, you play too fuckin' much!" I say and we all laugh. Mya and Ari go to the bar to get some drinks, walking hand in hand. They've been extra touchy with each other all night. I'm starting to think something's up between them, but I'll save that talk for another day.

"A ring *and* a baby on the way? Looks like you're getting your fairytale after all. Bitch, you deserve it, for real," Keisha says, now that we're alone.

"It's a good feeling. You know what they say when things seem too good to be true though," I tell her. "How's Lo feel about you being pregnant? We never talked about it."

"I don't know. It took him a minute to come around to the idea," she explains. "But the joke is on that nigga though," she says, catching me off guard.

"What you mean?" I ask, confused. She leans over and whispers something in my ear that makes my jaw drop. "Bitch, you lyin'!" She just raises an eyebrow at me.

We drop the conversation when Mya and Ari join us again. I don't know how this shit is gonna play out, but I do know it's not going to end well. None of that matters tonight though. It's my night. I have so many reasons to celebrate and that's what I'm 'bout to do. It's time for my girls and I to cut the fuck up. I walk to the dance floor and they follow my lead.

Chapter 17

Lo

The fog is thick in the air tonight, making it hard to see as Shine and I sit in silence in the blacked out Range Rover rental that's idling two houses down from the biggest lick of our lives. Whatever happens tonight, we'll have to take it to the grave - this will be a true test of loyalty. I look over at Shine as she looks ahead for any movement. We've been potnas for twelve years, so I already know when I move she's moving with me, no questions asked. I also know she's ready to put all this shit behind her, and I respect that. So tonight we're going big and then we're going home to live life to the fullest.

I can tell that Shine is in deep thought, so I nudge her arm pulling her back to the present. "Damn, my nigga, what you thinkin' 'bout over there? I know yo' ass ain't scared now," I tease her.

"Nah, bitch, I'm just ready to get this shit over wit' and get back to my girl," she responds, putting her phone in her pocket.

"Awww," I nudge her again, "shut the fuck up wit' all dat soft shit and hit this blunt, nigga. It'll take the edge off." I light the blunt that I had stored in the center console and pull hard from it a couple times, blowing smoke against the window shield.

"Nigga you always wanna get high," she laughs, "Pass that shit," she tells me, taking the blunt from me and hitting it. We sit in silence for a few more minutes, doing surveillance, and making sure there's no foot traffic. The dead end of 46th Street normally doesn't have much traffic, especially tonight when everybody's at Bella Noche to see that nigga Fredo Bang perform. Hopefully we'll be in and out of here fast enough that no one notices we left the club.

"So, when we gon' hit the spot? You know Mookie is already in there with that lame ass nigga. I'm ready to lay this nigga down after he beat the fuck out my cousin, bruh," I say, checking the time on my Apple watch; it's 10:55 PM.

Shine nods her head in agreement. "I ain't expecting nothin' less. Family is everything. I don't know what possessed Mookie's ol' dumb ass to start fuckin' with that street nigga anyway," she shakes her head in disappointment.

"She wanna be down and fit in," I explain, right as my phone vibrates alerting me that I have a text message. It's from Mookie. "Five more minutes. Mook said Rah Rah and his li'l brother, BJ, are down in the basement and she has Keno ducked off in a back bedroom. Let's hit this bitch and get the fuck outta here," I say, opening the driver's side door and creeping out into the night.

Shine follows my lead, exiting the Range and moving towards the trunk to the compartment where the guns are hidden. Normally Shine would carry her 9, but this job calls for something bigger, so I hand her the Tec-9. She pulls the strap over her shoulder and wraps the belt around the waist, loading the belt with full clips. I gotta be extra, so I pull out two Desert Eagles, one for each hand. Shine looks at me smirking and shaking her head, but she already knows I'm ready for whatever.

We move in silence up the side of the dead end street and cut through the grass around the side of the trap house. We make it to the back door and duck down when we see a figure coming towards the back door through the window. We ready our weapons, aiming them at the back door. Mookie opens the door wide, not surprised at all that guns are pointed in her face. She motions for us to come inside.

We step into what looks like a laundry room. "You sure you turned all the cameras and shit off?" Shine asks Mookie.

"Duh, bitch. You think you would've made it this far without him knowing if I hadn't?" she counters, hands on hips in defiance.

"You right. Now move out the fuckin' way. Where these niggas at?" Shine questions, making sure a full clip is secured in her gun.

"Keno is two doors to the left down this hallway. I told him I had to get some whip cream," she rolls her eyes. "Rah Rah and BJ are still in the basement. They been tryin' to hide everything from me, like a bitch green or sum'." We walked lightly down the hallway and Mookie pointed to a door at the end of the hall showing us the door that leads to the basement.

We move towards the door and push it open without a sound. Still stepping lightly, we creep down the stairs and notice that Rah Rah and BJ are sitting around a table laughing and talking shit while they count up stacks of money. We hit the bottom of the stairs, guns ready to fire, and they both jump up at the same time.

BJ attempts to go for his gun. "Don't try it, nigga," Shine's voice freezes him. "Get the fuck on the ground!" she demands.

Rah Rah laughs arrogantly. "Bitch, you better believe if you don't kill me I'm takin' out your whole muthafuckin' bloodline," he taunts.

Shine laughs in response. "I know how you move, nigga. You a dead man talkin' right now, and I don't fuck wit' the dead, so-" She doesn't even finish her sentence before she lights his ass up and his body drops to the ground. Blood pours from his bullet wounds creating a pool underneath his body.

"FUCK! Y'all really killed my fuckin' brother, mane. Fuck!" BJ is crying hysterically. His pussy ass ain't built for this shit. Hearing the noise, Keno makes his way down the stairs letting off a couple shots from his own hand gun. I turn quickly and lay his ass to rest before he makes it to the last step and his body rolls the rest of the way down. BJ is still in rare form, screaming and crying like a newborn baby.

"Bitch, you next," I tell BJ, irritated by his whining. "We just need the code to the safe. And we'll be takin' all this," I point my gun in the direction of stacks of money sitting on the table. Shine starts packing the money in duffle bags as BJ moves obediently towards the safe and begins putting in the code.

I turn away for a second to make sure Mookie is helping Shine load the money up, and don't notice BJ pull a gun out of the safe.

Pow!

Chapter 18

Shine

"**S**hit!" Lo grab's his arm as it bleeds profusely. Before I know it, I let off a round into BJ's body. The only thing on my mind is getting back to my queen. I am running out of patience with this shit. I drop my gun and rush over to Lo to see how badly the bullet punctured him. "I'm fine. I'm fine," he says, brushing me off. He may be right, but there was too much blood to be sure, so I sat him down in a chair.

"Just sit right here, nigga. Don't move," I order him. I'm pissed off now, because I have to load all this shit up on my own. I call Mookie downstairs to assist me and she rushes down immediately. As soon as she see's the blood covering Lo's arm she starts crying, which I don't have time for.

"Bitch, shut the fuck up wit' all that! He's fine. Take the keys," I toss her the keys to the Range Rover. "Bring the Range to the side door so we can load up. Hurry the fuck up!" She looks over to Lo, not quite believing he's okay.

"I'm okay Mook, go!" Lo confirms what I said, so she does as I asked. I grab two duffle bags and take the drugs off the safe, filling the bags up. Mook sends me a text that she's at the door, so I grab two bags and run them up the stairs out of the basement, then two more, and two more, until they are all out of the basement. "Nigga, hurry up! This shit hurts!" Lo hollers at me.

"Bitch, shut up! I'm short as fuck and I'm a whole fuckin' woman out here! How fast you want me to move, man?!" I toss the last two bags out the basement, and notice that Mookie has already started loading them into the car. I grab the last two and carry them out the door, around to the trunk of the Range, and throw them inside. "Get ready to pull off," I tell Mookie. "I gotta go help Lo's big ass."

When I make it back down the stairs, I see Lo bent over. I pull him up by his good arm and wrap it around my neck, holding him up with my other arm. "Come on, man. We gotta get the fuck outta here. The crew is on the way and we don't need nobody seeing us," I explain. We finally make it up the stairs and out of the house. I help him into the back seat and then make my way to the passenger seat. "We gotta get to Keshawn's apartment in Brookstown. I gotta stash this shit and get back to the club," I tell her.

Mookie pulls off onto 46th and before we make it to North Foster, I notice a familiar car moving toward us. As it gets closer, my thought is confirmed. It's Rah Rah's cousin, Gee.

They are headed to the trap and I know when Gee sees his cousin laid out, there's going to be smoke. When Gee makes eye contact with me and Mookie, I see two more of his potnas' cars pulling up at the intersection and somethin' tells me it's 'bout to be a warzone.

"Man, fuck!" I shout, hopping out the car, guns blazing in their direction. Bullets start flying back in my direction, but I hardly notice because my adrenaline's rushing. *Fuck! It wasn't supposed to go down like this,* I think. There are a few other cars in the street that either swerve out the way and speed forward or stop to see the action. When Gee and his people realize I ain't backing down, they let up, hop in their rides, and speed off. As soon as I get back in the car, Mookie hits the gas.

Nobody says a word during the short drive to my cousin's house. We pull up to her door and before the car is even in park I jump out and beat down my cousin's door. "Keshawn! Open the fuckin' door!" She swings the door open and when she sees us she doesn't ask any questions. "You and Mook get the shit out the trunk. I gotta get Lo. I hit up Doc on the way here, so he should pull up any minute," I explain to her. She immediately gets to work.

I help Lo inside the apartment and sit him in a chair at the kitchen table. "The doctor's on his way," I tell him. He nods his head before resting it on the table. I run to the back of the apartment and meet Mookie and Keshawn, using my key to let them in the back room where my safes are kept secured. "Just throw the shit in there. I gotta go," I tell them. "I'll come back for it later." Once all is secured in the room, I close the door and lock it behind me.

I rush out of the apartment, leaving Mookie with Lo, so that I can get rid of these guns and this car. When I get on the road I feel paranoid, because I don't know if anyone called the police about the shoot out. I head to Byron street, because I know them niggas in The Circle keep it solid. *I can get off this rental out there and walk to my car,* I think. When I make it to The Circle, I get out of the Range, douse the interior in gasoline, and set it ablaze. My car is parked one street over at my potna Tremaine's house, so I walk that way with the guns in a duffle bag over my shoulder.

When I make it to my car, I waste no time getting back on the road. I make it to Airline highway and head towards Port Allen, where there's a river for me to toss the guns after wiping them clean of any prints. Finally, I can get back to Nevaeh. *She's gonna kill me,* I think. I check my phone. It's fifteen minutes after midnight. *Yeah, she's definitely gonna kill me.*

I dial Keshawn's number. "How's Lo?" I ask her when she answers.

"Man, that nigga is fine after I fucked and sucked him real good," she replies.

"Bitch, that's too much fuckin' information, wit' yo' nasty ass," I say. "Tell him I'm headed back to the club and I'm gon' hit him up later." I end the call.

When I pull up to the club, I pull my Polo hoodie over my shirt to cover up the blood from Lo's bullet wound. It takes me no time to find Nevaeh in the crowd. I watch her for a moment while she and Keisha throw bills on Mya and Ari, who are dancing on each other seductively. Leave it to them hoes to put on a show. I make my way through the crowd to her.

"Baby, I was starting to think you left me here," she says, happy to see my face again.

"I'm here. You know I wouldn't leave you unattended for too long anyway," I soothe her worries, kissing her forehead. "You ready to go?"

"Yeah, let me tell the girls." She hugs each of her friends and thanks them for coming. The club's not as full as it was earlier, so the vibe is a little more settled. We walk out together, my arm around her shoulders, and head home.

***

"I started your bath water, babe," I say to Nevaeh as she walks into the bedroom and sits on the bed to unstrap her heels.

"You wanna join me?"

"No, I'm just gonna take a quick shower and let you soak while I order us some food and find a movie. It's after midnight, but I'm still celebrating you. We got a long night ahead of us, baby." I walk back into the master bathroom and pour rose water into the tub, then sprinkle rose petals on top of the water.

Nevaeh walks in behind me. "It smells good," she says, inhaling deeply. "This is beautiful. You really outdid yourself tonight." She starts stripping out of your clothes. Before I'm tempted to spread her legs open on the side of the tub, I kiss her lips and walk out of the bathroom.

In the guest bathroom, I strip out of my own clothes and throw them in a pile in the middle of the floor. I jump in the shower, applying Axe body wash to my bath towel and scrubbing my skin clean of all that took place tonight. After I wash my body a third time, I dry off and dress in a fitted white T-shirt and black and white Niké joggers, then wrap the pile of clothes in the towel I dried off with. I carry the clothes out to the terrace where there's a small grill. I lift the lid of the grill, throw the clothes inside, close the lid, and light it up.

Since Nevaeh's pregnant, she doesn't like for me to smoke inside, so I light up a blunt while she's in the tub. I sit back in one of the chairs on the terrace and blow smoke into the night, thankful to be home.

Once I make it back inside, I hear Nevaeh moving around in the bedroom, most likely to get dressed. I can't think of a place that I can order food this time of night, so I go to the pantry and pull out all the snacks I can find. Zebra Cakes, fudge Pop-tarts, cool ranch Doritos, and a box of Star Crunch. I find a bag of theater popcorn and put it in the microwave on two and a half minutes.

While I wait for the popcorn to finish popping, I walk over to the TV in the living room and see what movies are playing. The beeping of the microwave let's me know the popcorn is ready. Nights like this make me want to take Nevaeh to Vegas and marry her right away, so she doesn't slip out of the grasp. No matter what happens between us, I'll always cherish the time I get to spend with her by my side.

Chapter 19

Keisha

I left the club alone. Lo must have left at some point when I was with the girls and decided not to come back. I've been waiting up for him, because I was a little worried, but who am I kidding. That nigga does what the hell he wants to do, nothing has changed. I don't know why I wake up every day expecting shit to be different. I thought witnessing the love between Shine and Nevaeh on that stage tonight would've at least made him appreciate the love I give him. *The love his ass don't deserve,* I remind myself.

I call his phone again and he doesn't answer. I throw my phone at the front door with so much force that it shatters into pieces. *I'm fuckin' done with this nigga. When he walks in that fuckin' door I'm lettin' his ass have it,* I think. I storm off into the bedroom, taking all his clothes out of the dresser and throwing them into the trash bags. When I get to the last drawer, I hear him fumble his way into the apartment. *The nerve of this nigga.*

He walks into the bedroom and stops when he sees me packing all his shit up. "What the fuck are you doing, Keisha?" he asks.

"The fuck does it look like, nigga? You dipped out tonight without even letting me know to do what? Fuck some bitch and then think you 'bout to come lay in my bed?" I point to my queen-size bed. "Nah, nigga, it ain't goin' down like that. Look at you! You ain't even wearing the same clothes you was wearin' at the club. Where the fuck you been?"

"You don't want me to answer that, Ke."

"Oh, I don't want you to answer? 'Cause I don't need to know, right?" I ask, daring him to say the wrong thing. "Well, you wanna know somethin'?" I wait for him to answer when he doesn't I continue. "This ain't your fuckin' baby, you bitch ass nigga," I say casually, as if I'm giving him the weather report.

"What, bitch?" is all he says with rage in his eyes.

"Nigga, you heard me."

"I want you to repeat it," he says calmly.

"This. Ain't. Your. Baby." I spell it out to him again. He can act stupid if he wants to, but all I gotta do is make one call and his ass will be buried six feet under. *Well, shit, if I wouldn't have smashed my damn phone,* I think to myself.

"Who's the father, Keisha? Who's the baby for if it ain't mine, then?" he questions me, pacing back and forth. He walks toward the nightstand that's closest to the bedroom door, on his side of the bed. There's no way for me to get around him and there's no where for me to run to. I back away from him, towards the dresser. He reaches into the nightstand drawer and pulls out his hand gun. "WHO IS THE FUCKING BABY FOR, BITCH?!!" He raises his voice, causing me to jump.

I stand there shaking my head. If I tell him who the father is, I know he won't hesitate to pull the trigger. He pulls his phone out and dials a number. "Aye, I need a clean up... Yeah... At my girl's apartment... Nigga, don't ask no questions, just send someone," he hangs up the phone and puts it back in his pocket. "I'm gonna ask you again, who does this baby belong to?"

"Lo," I beg. "Please, you don't have to do this." He cocks the gun and places his finger on the trigger. "OK! OK! Rah Rah... Rah Rah is the father," I say, my voice quivering as I try to hold the tears back.

"Bitch, you were sleeping with the *enemy?!"*

"Lo, I can explain-" I say.

"Explain it to him," he interrupts.

"To him?"

"Yeah, when you meet that nigga in Hell. You *three* will be a big happy family. We killed that nigga tonight. When you see him, tell that bitch I said we're even," he says, knocking the breath out of me with each word.

I fall to my knees, cradling my stomach and crying out for my baby's father, for myself, and for my unborn child. "Lo, please," I beg once more.

"The time for all that shit is over, bitch. You're dead to me," he says as he pulls the trigger and everything goes completely black.

Chapter 20

Shine

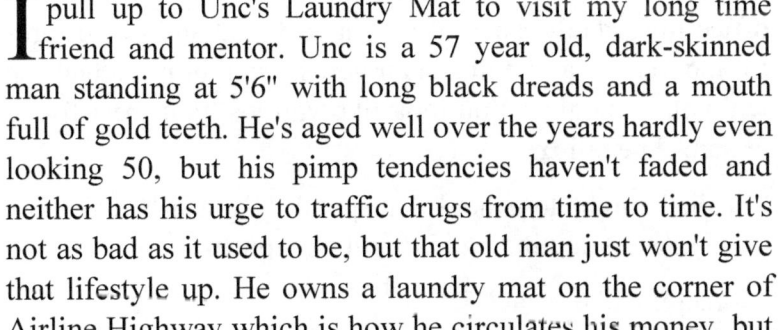

I pull up to Unc's Laundry Mat to visit my long time friend and mentor. Unc is a 57 year old, dark-skinned man standing at 5'6" with long black dreads and a mouth full of gold teeth. He's aged well over the years hardly even looking 50, but his pimp tendencies haven't faded and neither has his urge to traffic drugs from time to time. It's not as bad as it used to be, but that old man just won't give that lifestyle up. He owns a laundry mat on the corner of Airline Highway which is how he circulates his money, but it's also a spot that I go to clear my head and get shit off my chest. That man knows all my deepest and darkest secrets, but I know I never have to doubt whether he'll keep it real with me.

I don't have any clothes to wash, but I definitely need to air out this dirty laundry. I get out of my car and walk up to the entrance of the laundry mat, ringing the little bell above the door as I open it. I notice a couple of ladies loading clothes into washers and dryers and a man standing over the folding table to the left, folding his clean bed linen and placing it into a basket. "Unc! You in?" I yell.

Unc pokes his head up from behind the counter. "Didn't I tell you not to come in here hollering at me, nigga? You know my ass is gettin' old. These young kids don't have no damn manners these days," he fusses. "What brings you by?" he asks.

"I need to run it wit' you real quick," I tell him. When he doesn't move from behind the counter, I look around at all the people that are in the room with us. "Alone."

"Oh, step into my office," he says with a playful tone, although this is no laughing matter. I follow him into his office towards the back of the laundry mat and he gestures for me to have a seat in a chair across from him. "What's up wit' you, youngin'? You look like you lost your best friend or sum'," he tells me.

"Yeah, I might lose her." I respond. "I got a bad feeling, man. Like something bad is 'bout to happen."

"Somethin' like what?"

"I don't know... like I might go to jail..." I say, looking down at the floor.

"Nigga, pick your damn head up. What the hell happened? I thought you gave all that shit up? His expression is scrunched up in confusion and he narrows his eyes at me.

"Yeah, I did give it up. Nevaeh made me promise her that I wouldn't put us at risk anymore," I confess. "But Lo hit me up and wanted me to hit this last lick with him for two mil' and I couldn't let him go in that water alone. But that ain't even the problem, man. I was being careless. Rah Rah's people hemmed us up and I got out the car and had a shoot out with them niggas in the middle of the street." I shake my head in disappointment at my own self, so I don't even look up to see Unc's face. I know he's just as disappointed in me, if not more.

"His cousin definitely seen us. And there were a few cars in the street, so someone else could have seen me and might be able to identify me. It was right in front the traffic light and I know there's cameras and shit. I just wasn't thinking clearly. Everything just happened so fast," I tell him. I look up at him now, regretting it immediately, not because he looks mad, but because he looks worried. "Nevaeh will never forgive me for this shit. I fucked up."

"Did you tell her?"

"No, I didn't tell her. That's why I'm here. I don't know what to do or what to say. She's pregnant and she's already high risk. I don't wanna stress her. I just want this shit to go away," I answer him.

"Well, it probably won't happen like that. The good things always happen too slowly and the bad things happen too quickly. It definitely sounds like it could've been worse, but I'd say your best bet right now would be heading home and spending time with your woman. Tell her the truth. Let her choose to stand by your side, don't force her to be along for the ride because you kept her in the blind. She has proven she can handle the real from you. You owe her that," he lectures me. Normally I hate being lectured, but the old man is right.

"You made your bed and you know what happens next - you gotta lay in it. I know that's not what you wanna hear, but I'm not 'bout to sugar coat it for you. Nigga, you got a baby on the way. How you gon' take care of a baby from behind bars?" he inquires.

"I-"

"You can't. Even if you find a way to provide for them, it won't be legal. And that's not what you need right now. You young niggas need to start thinking before y'all get all trigger happy," he says. "Go home, Shine. Get your affairs in order and go talk to your woman. You ain't gotta give her all the details, but tell her enough so that she knows what to prepare for. Like I said, give her a choice."

"You're right, Unc. I'm gon' make this shit right," I tell him, standing from my seat. He stands as well, patting my back with his hand. "Thank you for taking the time out for me, I know you be busy pimpin' and shit," I laugh.

"Aye, don't hate, nigga. Pimpin' ain't easy these days. Hoes awalys tryna have their own mind and be all independent and shit. It's more trouble than it's worth," he laughs with me. "I always got time to spare for you. You know how to hit my line if you need me," he says, holding the door to his office open for me as I walk through it.

"See you later, old man," I say, leaving the laundry mat. I turn back just in time to see him flip me off for calling him old and laugh on my way to the car. I don't know how Nevaeh is going to take this, but I know I have to do right by her. I get in my car and speed home to her, hoping she's in a forgiving mood.

Chapter 21

Nevaeh

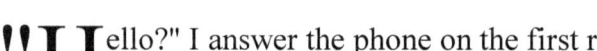

"Hello?" I answer the phone on the first ring.

"Hey sweetheart, how you doing?"

"I'm doing okay, Mama. How 'bout you?" Hearing my mama's voice puts a smile on my face instantly.

"I'm good. Just wanted to call and check on you. I hear you're getting married?" she inquires.

"Yes ma'am. Shine proposed last night at the birthday party she threw for me. How'd you find out?" I ask.

"Well, you know she's old-fashioned and beyond her years. When y'all last visited us she pulled your daddy to the side and asked his permission to marry his daughter," she says. I almost drop the phone in disbelief that Shine would go to that extent for me. "And he said as long as she keeps you safe and happy, he gives his blessing."

"Wow, I had no idea."

"That girl loves you, Vae. She seems like a keeper to me. I'm happy for you two," she says. "Go be happy, baby girl. Marriage is through thick and thin, but I have a feeling that both of you can stand the rain."

"Thank you, Mama. I love you. Tell Daddy I love him, too. We'll be out to see y'all soon," I look out the window to see Shine's Charger coming up the road. "Shine's pulling up now, so I'm gonna go get dinner ready," I tell her.

"Okay, baby. We love you," she replies and ends the call. I don't know where I'd be without my parents. I really appreciate how supportive they've been of my relationship with Shine. I walk eagerly to the door to open it and let Shine inside.

"Hey, babe," she greets me, kissing my lips before passing me by to get into the house.

"Hey... Why do you seem like you're in a rush?" I ask. She doesn't bother to take her shoes off before heading straight for the kitchen. "Shine?" I follow her into the kitchen. "Baby, what's wrong? Did something happen?"

"I have some things I need to tell you. Just please hear me out. You'll probably be angry with me, but just know that everything I do, I do because I want us to be straight and have the life we've always wanted," she explains, her words jumbling together as if she can't get them out quick enough.

"Shine, just tell me what's going on. Please." I try to keep my tone calm, but my anxiety is raising as the minutes pass. I don't know what she's gotten herself into, but from the sound of it, it isn't good. Stress is not good for the baby, so I keep breathing steady.

As Shine explains everything to me, from start to finish, I fight tears from falling from my eyes. When I met Shine, this was her lifestyle. Though I made her promise me that she would put it all behind her so that we can have a family, I knew there was a chance that she'd be pulled back into it eventually. I hoped she'd resist it, but I know how loyal she is to her friend.

I walk around to the kitchen table and sit in the chair next to her. "Look at me," I say, my voice calm. She meets my eyes and I can see the remorse in her eyes from feeling like she has let me down. "We're gonna get through this, OK? No matter what happens, I'll be here. And whatever I can do to help, I will." I take her hands in mine and squeeze them. "I need you. And this baby needs you. So, I need you to pull yourself together and tell me what needs to be done."

We sit at the table and talk about the possible outcomes and what affairs we need to get in order. I leave the table to get us each a bottle of water from the refrigerator. Before I make it back to the table, there's a knock at the door. Shine looks up at me, closes her eyes and shakes her head. The knocking gets louder and more persistent. I move to look out the blinds and see that we are surrounded by flashing blue lights, just as I thought.

"Open up!" a voice comes from outside. "B.R.P.D.! Open up or we're coming in!" the voice demand.

"Shine..." I say, a tear falling from my eye.

"Vae, don't you fuckin' cry. I need you to be strong. I love you; just know that I love you more than anything. I'm gonna make it back to you, Nevaeh. On everything, I will make it back to you and the baby," she embraces me so tightly I can hardly breathe.

"I love you more," I say to her. She walks toward the door and opens it, walking out with her hands above her head. The officer grabs her immediately and turns her around, pulling both of her hands behind her back and throwing her against the cop car. He roughly places handcuffs around her wrists. "Shyanne Harris, you are under arrest for the illegal use of a firearm and three counts of attempted murder. You have the right to remain silent. Anything you say can and will be used against you in a court of law. You have the right to an attorney. If you can not afford an attorney, one will be appointed to you..." The officer's voice fades into the background as I watch them take my fiancé away and throw her in the back of the cop car.

As they drive away with her, I go back into the house and close the door behind me. "FUCK!" I slam my fists against the door. I walk back to the kitchen to find my phone and search through my contacts until I find the number I need.

"Dominique, that favor you owe me - I'm callin' it in," I say when she answers. "I'm on my way."

Acknowledgments:

First and foremost, we want to thank God for providing the ideas, thoughts, motivation, and tools we needed to start and finish this project. Our circumstances maybe seem bleak, but You always show up and show out for us and we are thankful for your blessings and grace in our lives.

We'd like to thank our families, friends, and others who've genuinely given support and encouragement in our journey - you know who you are! You all may have been more excited to see the finished project than we were. Thank you for believing in us along the way.

Last but not at all least, we want to give a special thanks to George and Ken for saving the day and pushing Cadmus Publishing LLC to new heights. We are truly grateful for the assistance, input, and encouragement you have given us. You've treated this project as if it were you're own. Thank you so much for that.

ABOUT THE AUTHOR

Dashay Denise is a duo of female writers that met while both were incarcerated. During that time, they joined minds, putting idle time to use, to venture into the urban genre, creating a novel that demonstrates the tragedies of life as well as a love that is passionately dangerous.

47907CB00007B/2272

*9 7 8 1 6 3 7 5 1 4 4 4 3 *